THE DIAMONDS

AURUM REGIUM

Made with ♥ on the Notion Press Platform
www.notionpress.com

Contents

Contents

Prologue

Rain was falling from the sky in sheets and the sea was on a high tide. The soft patter of the raindrops was contrasted yet complemented by the loud noise of the crashing waves. A man was standing on the balcony of a large and beautifully built house facing towards the sea. Holding a cup of coffee in his hand, he was looking around him with an air of authority. The man was the owner of the lush green, tropical island where the house was situated. This ownership was a legacy left behind by his parents, a legacy that he was carrying forward. The only other inhabitants of the island were a group of tribals who had been associated with the family since they had bought the island, generations ago, and permitted the tribals to live as they were living before the island was purchased. This act had touched the hearts of the tribals, and they had begun to see the family as a part of their own group.

The man was staring at the waves when suddenly, his attention was caught by the sound of someone entering the large sitting room behind him. Two people had entered the sitting room and had sat down on the comfortable couch. The man walked in and sat on the large armchair facing the two people. He smiled a little.

He placed the now empty cup of coffee on the table and addressing the latest arrivals to the room, he said, "You obviously have a lot of questions and rest assured, all of them will be answered. The only condition is that you listen to what I am about to tell you with rapt attention and without any interruptions. By the end, you will know it all and quite frankly, it will leave you dumbstruck."

The man smiled again and began his narrative. An extraordinary narrative, the likes of which nobody had ever heard before.

CHAPTER ONE

A man wearing a smart suit was grunting and struggling with the tie around his neck. The overall appearance of the man was quite remarkable. He was six feet one inch tall with piercing brown eyes and brown hair which was speckled with grey, and this was one of the most prominent signs of his age. Although the man was not very old, around forty-five, but he made no attempt whatsoever to look younger, as many would do. In fact, he believed that his age was an indication of his wisdom and experience, the two things he was extremely proud of.

After a struggle of five more minutes, the man had still not succeeded against the tie. To his relief, he saw the reflection of a beautiful woman in her mid-forties, his wife, Martha Brown, enter the room and he turned towards her, arms spread in an act of defeat.

The woman laughed a little and assisting her husband with the tie, she said, "I have lost count of the years since you are trying *and failing*, to learn to tie this thing properly."

The man looked at his reflection in the mirror and proudly adjusted the perfectly knotted tie that sat around his neck. "No big deal. It is said that Einstein didn't even like tying his own shoelaces."

The woman folded her arms and said, "Maybe. But he didn't have to outwit murderers and crooks for a living."

The man turned towards his wife with an alarmed expression and said, "Oh please! I work for the FBI, but you make it sound like I am a thug!"

The woman laughed again. "All right, Special Agent Jefferson Brown, don't forget your wallet."

The man patted his pocket and said, "Of course not...Where is it?"

His wife held it up and the man took it and put it in his pocket gratefully. He bid goodbye to his wife and was soon sitting in his car, en route to his office. As he saw the people on the streets of New York, he could not help but wonder what a fantastic city he lived in. Everyone was focused on themselves, some were working, some were on the phone, while others were just hurrying along. When looked upon individually, these people did not seem to be special, but when viewed as a whole, they were responsible for making NYC the splendid city that it was.

Agent Brown reached his office and exchanged a few friendly words with his colleagues. Everyone respected him and most of the younger agents idolized him. This was due to the fact that the Agent had a stellar record. Never in his career had he come across a case which he could not bring to a successful conclusion. Although each case of his was a success, but his most renowned one was one of his earliest cases. It was a case that had tested him to his limits and after the completion of which, there was little doubt to the abilities of the man. In fact, people quoted that incident to emphasize the point that nothing was impossible. From then on, sky was the limit and Jefferson had become a part of the FBI's best agents.

Jefferson entered his office and sat down on his desk. There was a lot of work to be done and a lot of bad guys to be caught. He dove into the files which were stacked in a neat pile on one corner of his desk and was soon engrossed in the details of the case.

There are three types of people in the world- the ones who work to earn money, the ones who work to pass the time and the ones who work as they love what they do. Jefferson was one of the rare people who fell into the last category. Since as early as he could remember, he had always wanted to pursue a career in law enforcement. He was the first in his family to have chosen to be an officer of the law and it was evident that it was a phenomenal choice on his part.

Suddenly, there was a knock on the door of Jefferson's office. After receiving the permission to enter, a smart young man with blond hair and blue eyes entered. Jefferson recognized the man instantly as Samuel Reed. He was one of the young men whose presence assured everyone that the future of the bureau was in safe hands. Agent Reed was disciplined, focused, fearless and had a practical and methodical mind, that is to say, he had all the qualities that assured a successful career with the FBI.

Agent Brown looked at Reed and said, "Good morning, Sam. What have you got for me?"

Sam shook his head and said, "How many times have I requested you not to call me Sam?"

"Why not?" asked Jefferson innocently, although he knew the answer to his question very well.

"Because *Sam* makes it sound like I am a little child, not an FBI agent," said Sam as though he was tired of repeating it.

Jefferson chuckled. "Very well, now, tell me what brings you to me."

Sam did not answer. Rather, he looked as though he was about to say something that he did not want to. After a while of uncomfortable silence, however, the young agent mustered up courage and decided to speak up.

"We've received an anonymous tip," said Sam.

Jefferson raised an eyebrow and said, "About what?"

"About a robbery. They say a specific set of diamonds is going to be stolen."

"They?" asked Jefferson.

"Could be a man or a woman, an untraceable call was received early morning today and the voice was mechanically disguised," explained Sam.

"Which set of diamonds?" asked Jefferson.

Sam was silent once again. His eyes expressed a lot more than what was possible using words.

"Which set, Sam?"

Sam looked at Jefferson straight in the eyes and said, "*Les morceaux de lumière.*"

Les morceaux de lumière, widely considered to be one of the most precious and purest diamonds in the world. Their name, which translated to "The pieces of light", was the aptest name for the diamonds. They reflected light with such intensity that it appeared as though they were *radiating* light. The five diamonds were cut with utmost precision and dated back to the times when even the sight of diamonds was a privilege that could only be enjoyed by the very rich. Throughout the years, they had ended up in one private collection or another. Some owners were smart, and they did not boast, nor did they announce what they had acquired, others freely advertised their pride and thus, they were under the constant fear of the diamonds being stolen. However, except once, this fear had never taken the form of reality, as the security measures taken to protect the diamonds were the best. But the reason, why Sam was so nervous and why he expected Jefferson to react strongly to this piece of news, was that this set of diamonds held a special place in the agent's life. *Les morceaux de lumière* were at the very center of the case which had laid the foundation for what Jefferson had achieved.

Jefferson had not replied. His face had gone lax, and his eyes seemed to go out of focus for an instant. Seconds later, he regained his composure and laughed. Sam looked at him incredulously, his expression conveyed the message that he had a slight suspicion that the man in front of him had lost his senses.

Jefferson noticed Sam's expression and said, "Why are you looking at me with that expression on your face?"

"How can you laugh at something like that?" asked Sam.

"Oh, come on! If I claim that I will be robbing the Swiss bank tomorrow, that does not mean that I can," said Jefferson in a matter-of-fact way.

"Are you telling me that you think it's a hoax?"

"To be quite honest, I am quite surprised that you believe such claims. You know as well as I do that the security of those diamonds is impenetrable."

"But as I recall, someone came very close once."

Now Jefferson's smile faded. "And as I recall, they are behind bars now."

Sam said, "Very well, as you say."

After precisely twenty-seven minutes had passed, there was another knock on Jefferson's door. There was a parcel for him. There was no name on the package and according to the delivery man, it had been left at the entrance of the building with Jefferson's name on it. A metal detector test had been done and the package had undergone the scanner. Jefferson opened the package. There was a single chit of paper within it, the chit had a single line printed across it and when Jefferson read it, he crumpled the paper and took a sip of water. He ran a hand through his hair and sat down on his desk. The single line had forced Jefferson to reconsider a decision of his.

Outside Jefferson's office, in the bullpen, Sam was sitting in his cubicle. A file was open on the desk in front of him, but Sam was staring at the screen of his computer. He was researching about *Les morceaux de lumière*. Suddenly, Jefferson entered the cubicle and looked at Sam's screen.

For a moment, Sam was flustered, then he said, "What's up?"

Agent Brown said, "We need to inspect the security of the diamonds."

"Why the sudden change of heart?"

In reply, Jefferson handed Sam a crumpled piece of paper. There was only a single line printed on the chit, but it was enough to make Sam realize the gravity of the situation. The line read - *Les morceaux de lumière will be stolen soon.*

CHAPTER TWO

Agent Michael Adams was running towards the gate of the federal building. The casual onlooker would have seen a young man who was six feet tall, had a fit physique with jet-black hair and eyes such a dark shade of brown that they appeared black, along with a beard which was a sign of avoiding the blade for more than thirty-six hours. The man looked tired, and his skin was even paler than usual, but it was his eyes that indicated his alert state of mind. Once inside, he flashed his badge at the security guard and ran towards the elevator. He knew that he was late for work, and this was not unusual now. The past year had been difficult. He didn't even remember the last time he had reached work on time. Just as he reached the cubicle and dumped his bag on the desk, he realized that he was extremely sleepy. He needed to get some caffeine to keep himself awake. He walked to the coffee machine, there was another agent there, but she looked at Michael once, then turned her gaze away and left. Michael did not react, by now he was used to such cold behavior on his colleagues' part. There was a time when he had a lot of friends, and everyone was helpful, but now, he felt as though he was alone.

Michael did not even despise the others for the way they behaved with him. This was because he knew that he was the one to be blamed for what had happened, it was due to his own mistakes, his own lack of control, that he had lost not one but multiple chances to achieve success in life. Now, he knew that everyone thought of him as a lost cause.

Michael was sipping his coffee when Sam came into his field of vision. It appeared he had just had a talk with Agent Brown after which he hurried out of the bullpen and was soon out of sight. Michael shook his head and sat down on his chair. He opened a file and tried to focus on work. After two minutes he closed the file with a sigh. The will to work seemed to have vanished from Michael's life. Whenever he began working, a single thought made him lose all desire to proceed and the thought was that no matter how hard he worked, he would never be able to achieve the success which had been previously easy for him. This conclusion of his was the result of the realization that no one in the entire bureau trusted his capabilities anymore. Instead of being someone they could rely on, he was now perceived as a liability for the entire unit.

Opening a book of sudoku puzzles, Michael settled comfortably in his chair and spent a happy fifteen minutes playing with the numbers. At the end of this period, however, he had to leave the puzzle as he realized that Sam was back in his cubicle. Try as we might, there is an incessant desire of humans to know what others have been up to. It is an almost irrepressible part of the human nature, and it was to follow this very urge that Michael got up from his seat and went into Sam's cubicle.

Sam looked at Michael and his expression changed at once. He looked as though he did not want to talk to Michael, but he was finding it difficult to find a way to make him go away.

Michael said, "Hello Sam."

"Hello, Michael."

Further troubled by Sam's unenthusiastic response, Michael said, "I just saw that you had a word with Agent Jefferson, I was just wondering what you talked about."

"Nothing much," said Sam, although his tone made it feel like he wanted to say – 'None of your business'.

"Please Sam, I'm just curious," said Michael with a strained voice. "Nobody ever tells me anything anymore."

These words convinced Sam to loosen his tongue. He had an exceedingly kind heart and could not bear to look at someone in trouble or in distress.

He said, "We received an anonymous tip this morning, a claim that *Les morceaux de lumière* will be stolen soon."

Now it was Michael's turn to look surprised, and excited. "You aren't telling me you believed that?"

"That is sort of what I did but Agent Jefferson was convinced that it was a hoax until..."

"Until what?"

"Until he received a package and inside lay a single chit of paper." Saying this Sam handed Michael the crumpled piece of paper which he had received from Agent Jefferson.

Michael read it once and then read it again, then he looked at Sam and said, "So what has Jefferson decided to do now?"

"Well, first of all, we are going to visit David Wood's place to check the security of the diamonds," replied Sam.

Now, an idea came into Michael's head, an idea which seemed to have little chances of being successful but if it was, then there might still be a future for him at the FBI. He thanked Sam, almost ran out of the cubicle and knocked on the door of Agent Jefferson's office. After receiving the permission to enter, he walked in and closed the door behind him, making sure that the voices of the people within the room could not escape to the outside.

Agent Jefferson was staring at Michael as though he had seen him for the first time. Over the last year, Michael had become isolated to the extent that sometimes the agent did not see him for days on end. Agent Jefferson believed that this was because Michael was ashamed of what had happened and thus, he did not want to face his colleagues. The senior agent still remembered how Michael used to be, lively, focused and quite extraordinary. He had the gift of linking seemingly unrelated pieces of evidence, which in turn enabled him to direct his investigation in the right direction. He had achieved a few early successes in his career, and consequently, he had been labelled as one of the most promising agents in the bureau.

Everything had been on the perfect track for the young agent but then, after spending just two years as an FBI agent, his struggle with alcohol addiction had begun. It started with just a glass of wine in the evening to relax himself, but soon it proceeded to an entire bottle and even further. In no time at all, Michael had started showing signs of alcohol addicts, he had lost focus and due to the same, he had failed miserably in some cases. Over time, his steep descends had made him land at the rock bottom and that was where he was now, considered to be utterly useless and devoid of potential. But the most disturbing part was that Michael still believed that he did not need any external help to conquer his addiction and so far, he had failed. Every glass was filled with the promise of being the last, but the promise was broken as soon as the container was drained.

Michael said, "Good morning, Jefferson."

"Good morning."

"I was just talking to Sam and..." Michael's voice trailed off.

"And what?"

"And he told me that you had received a tip that the *Les morceaux de lumière* will be stolen."

"Yes, but the authenticity of that tip is quite questionable."

"But you are still going to check on the security arrangements, aren't you?"

Jefferson shifted in his seat a little and said, "I am just going to warn the owner."

Michael sat down on one of the chairs, an act which received a raised eyebrow from Jefferson.

"I just wanted to say that I would like to be a part of the case."

Michael's direct approach was unexpected and thus, Jefferson took a moment before replying.

"Michael, I would be very frank with you. I don't think that's a promising idea."

"Look, I know what you all think of me. You think I am a worthless drunk, but I deserve a second chance!"

Jefferson looked up sharply and said, "As I recall Agent, you received quite a lot of these *second chances*."

"I know, but I *need* another one, I need it to prove that I am not done yet, that I still have potential!"

Jefferson was silent. He knew what Michael was going through, but he did not want to take a risk by allowing Michael to collaborate with him. He believed that alcohol addiction made a person untrustworthy, and that was not a characteristic of a good partner. Agent Jefferson decided to go for the subtle approach.

"Agent Reed is already working on the case with me, if I need further assistance, I will surely call upon you."

Michael was still not satisfied. He was constantly twisting his hands which was a sign of his excessive nervousness.

"Please, I am requesting you, I need another chance. I swear I'll prove my worth to you! I know my next mistake would be my last one, but I assure you that I would not commit one!"

Now Agent Jefferson was annoyed. He had tried the tactical and gentle approach, but perhaps what Michael needed was the hard truth. "Michael, I cannot work with someone who is under the control of the bottle."

Michael was taken aback. He opened and closed his mouth a few times, but no sound escaped his lips. He swallowed but was still having trouble speaking. Agent Jefferson took this as a sign that the conversation was over, he turned his attention towards his computer and pretended to forget that Michael was in the office.

After a moment, a voice reached his ears. "What if I told you that I would leave it?"

Now agent Jefferson looked at Michael with new interest.

"Leave what?"

"Leave drinking. Forever. I would not even touch the bottle again if you give me another chance," said Michael, with such conviction that Agent Jefferson was moved.

There was silence for an entire minute after these words were spoken. Varied thoughts were going through the men's minds. Agent Jefferson was aware that if Michael kept the promise he had just made then he could still make a career for himself, however, he was not entirely sure if Michael could manage to be successful in his battle against alcohol. He knew stronger men who had tried and failed. On the other hand, Michael was not sure if he could stay true to what he had just said, but one thing was clear in Michael's mind, *He would try his best.*

Finally, Agent Jefferson said, "Very well Michael, one chance. But remember, if you mess up, I will have to ask you to leave."

"Thank you so much!" said Michael and sprang up to his feet. Even if he tried, he could not explain what he was feeling, it was joy, excitement so intense that he could feel his skin tingling. He felt as if he finally had a chance to achieve what he had always wanted.

After Michael had exited the office, Agent Jefferson interlaced his fingers and fell into deep thought. *Les morceaux de lumière* were extremely precious diamonds with the best security arrangements. It would be extremely hard to steal them but then, as Sam had said, someone had come remarkably close once. In fact, the diamonds *had* been stolen and it was Agent Jefferson himself who had recovered them. It seemed like a lifetime ago, but Agent Jefferson still remembered the details of that case as though it was yesterday. Two thieves, the best of their time, had successfully stolen the diamonds, they had even murdered the owner in the process but that was the accident, or so they claimed, but for some reason, Jefferson had believed them. He had caught the thieves and recovered the diamonds within 72 hours and that was the case that had earned him fame in the bureau. The diamonds had been returned to the original owner's son and that was where they were presently.

Jefferson came out of the office after some time and was met by Sam. The former said, "Sam! Did you arrange a meeting for us?"

"Yep, I was just coming to your office, we are due there in the late afternoon," said the young agent.

"Good. There is something else, I have asked Michael..."

Sam cut in and said, "I know, he told me himself. He is too happy for words, I don't even remember the last time I saw him like this."

Agent Jefferson did not say anything, but he hoped that everything went well.

After travelling a considerable distance, at precisely 4 PM that day, three FBI agents rang the doorbell of David Wood's house. To call the residence of David Wood a house was the same as calling a football field a park. It was wrong, simply wrong. David Wood owned a mansion which was surrounded by a beautiful lawn. The mansion was built to provide the residents with utmost comfort and the Wood family would have settled for nothing less than the best.

David Wood was the son of the late Robert Wood, who was a business tycoon. His son had followed in his father's footsteps and had taken his business to greater heights and now it appeared, his daughter was also following the same path as she was greatly interested in business as well. David had never forgotten what Agent Jefferson had done for his family and thus, he looked upon him as a great friend. The FBI had been involved in the case initially because the thieves who had attempted to steal *Les morceaux de lumière* were internationally famous for committing near impossible robberies. They always left behind the same sign, two interlaced silver rings of unequal sizes. This was the same sign which had drawn the attention of Agent Jefferson towards the original case.

Now, as the agents were let into the villa by a butler, they could not help but admire the rich taste in which the accommodations of the billionaire had been constructed and furnished. The man himself was seated on a beautiful armchair in the sitting room. The first impression which anyone formed about David Wood was that of a man about the same age as agent Jefferson and who had an expensive taste in clothes and watches. He had brown eyes and black hair in which streaks of grey were clearly visible. The overall manner of the man was smart and one that left a lasting impression in everyone's mind.

Just as David saw Agent Jefferson, he stood up and extending his hand, he said, "Jefferson! A pleasure as always!"

Agent Jefferson grasped the hand and giving it a brief shake, he said, "I am not quite sure you would hold on to that statement once we tell you why we are here."

Everyone sat down once the introductions were made. Michael kept the bag he was carrying beside him and comfortably settled on the sofa. Although physically present in the room, Michael's mind was elsewhere. He was trying to assess and calculate the standards of the security of the villa based on what he had seen so far. There had been armed guards at the main gate and the entire property was protected with alarm equipped electrical fences. Although that was quite good, Michael had already figured out a few ways to beat that. While one involved bribing the guard in the control room, another one did not involve any other person at all, the thief would just require some gadgets and he would be in.

Next were the CCTV cameras. Although he was not told, but Michael was sure that they ran in a closed-circuit network and thus hacking them would not be easy, unless you did it from within the network. During the time of the shift change there was a window of five to seven minutes in the evening when there was no one monitoring the cameras. A thief in peak physical conditions could manage to get over the fence and then put the video feed of the cameras on a loop within that interval of time. He had thought this far when Michael saw that Agent Jefferson was explaining the situation to David.

Agent Jefferson said, "David, I would not hide anything from you. We are here because we have received a tip that someone will try to steal *Les morceaux de lumière*."

"But that is not easy, Jefferson. You know it as well as I do, there is not one flaw in the security," replied David with some pride as he sipped the whisky in his hand.

Jefferson was about to reply when Michael spoke up. "I'm afraid that's not true."

All heads turned towards Michael instantly.

"Care to elaborate?" said David, with a hint of sarcasm.

"Certainly..." replied Michael and he went on to shed light on the security flaws which he had discovered so far, "... and that, I am sure, is not all."

Now the confidence of the billionaire seemed to have gone down a notch. Initially he had been taking the matter lightly, but now there was slight worry in his voice when he said, "So what do you suggest we do?"

Michael looked at Jefferson, but the latter remained silent and stared back. The meaning of this refusal to speak was evident, Michael had laid forth the problems and he was the one who was expected to have the solutions.

Michael cleared his throat and said, "I believe the easiest way to deal with the problems would be to solve the latter one. If there would be a guard monitoring the CCTV cameras and the security footage at all times, then there would be no chance of anyone even getting over the fence. The simplest way to achieve this is to hire at least one more guard whose sole job would be to watch over the CCTV cameras at odd times such as late night, early morning or during shift changes."

Jefferson was impressed. He said, "That's a good suggestion. Simple and effective."

David also agreed to the same and the conversation soon shifted to the security of the room where the diamonds were stored. The owner of the estate took the agents to the location in question, and everyone was momentarily stunned by the sight of the sparkling diamonds. They indeed appeared to *radiate* light rather than *reflect* it.

The room could only be opened by a special key card which was possessed only by one of Mr. Wood's most trusted guards who was stationed outside the door of the room for the greater part of the day. At night, another equally trustworthy guard would take over and these two were the only ones, apart from the Wood family, who had access to the room. Their behavior and actions were strictly monitored by the CCTV camera right overhead and thus, even if they wanted to, they could not take any menacing action. The room itself was completely sealed and ventilation and temperature control were managed by small air ducts. The diamonds were encased in a bulletproof glass case that was pressure sensitive.

Overall, there seemed to be no major security flaws and stating the same in an informal manner Sam said, "I'm sure this place is a thief's nightmare."

Mr. Wood gave a small smile at this appreciative remark. Even Jefferson expressed his satisfaction with the security and Michael followed suit. With nothing left to do, the agents took their leave and left behind a worried business tycoon.

Once inside the car, Sam said, "The security of that place is top notch, I don't think we need to arrange for extra security?"

"Are you saying he should not hire another guard?" asked Jefferson.

"Oh, that was not what I meant, I was talking about federal security. There is no need to make any arrangements, is there?"

"Not at the moment, After all, all we have to go on is a single chit of paper."

Until now, Michael had been silent, but now he looked up and said, "But what if the claim is true? We might need extra security then, as a single extra guard won't suffice."

Jefferson said, "Well, I think that at the moment, the diamonds are quite secure."

"Speaking of the chit, did they try to find out who had left the package for you?" asked Sam

"They tried, but the thing is that the package was hand delivered, so there is not much to investigate," replied Jefferson.

"What about the CCTV footage?" asked Sam.

"We do have someone, just a hooded figure, they can't even tell the gender of the suspect through that recording."

"So, what do we do next?" asked Michael.

Jefferson was silent for a moment, then he said, "All we can do is wait."

CHAPTER THREE

As Jefferson had said, for the next few days the trio of federal agents did nothing but wait impatiently, but nothing happened. Every call was received with anticipation but when it turned out that the call was not even remotely related to the diamonds, the enthusiasm ebbed away. For a week, nothing happened, neither at the bureau nor at the Wood Residence. The diamonds were safe, and the recommended arrangements had been made. A new guard had been hired whose sole purpose was to monitor the cameras and the security during the odd hours. Every letter or package for Agent Jefferson was monitored but nothing of interest came up.

Jefferson had begun to feel that it was wrong of him to act just based on an anonymous tip. After all, it could be just a spoof, someone with a twisted sense of humor making the FBI run around just for a laugh. Such thoughts were the major contributors to the elevation of Jefferson's stress levels. On the other hand, Sam and Michael were not comfortable working with each other but individually, each one of them was keeping an eye on what went on at the Wood residence.

On the morning of the eighth day, Jefferson entered his office with a determined expression. He had decided to call David Wood and inform him that the claim of the diamonds being stolen was not true. He was about to pick up his phone when his mobile rang. The call was from David Wood.

Agent Brown said, "Hello David, I was just about to call you. Listen, about the claim that the diamonds will be stolen, I think..."

The impatient voice of David cut in and he shouted, "It has happened, Jefferson! The diamonds have been stolen!"

"What! When?" asked Jefferson.

"Last night."

Jefferson did not waste any more time, he disconnected the call, informed Michael, and Sam about the robbery and within four minutes, they were on their way to the crime scene. Once they reached their destination, they were greeted by a distressed David Wood who did not look anything like the smart gentlemen they had met just over a week ago. Now, David was a nervous wreck.

Jefferson said, "Come on David, pull yourself together, tell me everything."

"There *is* nothing to tell!" said David "Last night, before going to bed, I checked the diamonds myself and they were quite all right, and today morning they were gone while the guard outside the door lay unconscious."

Sensing that the billionaire was clueless about how the robbery had taken place, Jefferson asked Sam and Michael to do a quick check of the CCTV footage and the security. The young agents left and were soon working and communicating perfectly. Both of them understood that even if they were not fond of each other, when there was work to be done, they had to put their differences aside and work as a team. And they did. They went over as much CCTV footage as they could, and they even checked if any alarms had been tripped but none of those incidents had taken place. The entire security staff was summoned and they were questioned if they saw something out of ordinary, but every individual gave the same answer, no one knew anything.

Walking up to Jefferson, Sam said, "Nothing. There is nothing to find, the CCTV footage had been looped somehow, and the alarms had been shut down. There was no evidence left behind and we have no idea how they did it."

Michael said, "They looped the CCTV footage, which means they somehow gained access to the system, we need IT to go over it immediately."

Jefferson nodded. "I have already called for the team. I have asked them to start from the lawn. I wanted to be the first one to check the room where the diamonds were kept."

David Wood led the way up to the room in question and opened the door with a spare security card in his possession. The guard who had been posted outside the room was the one in possession of the original key and since he was knocked out, there was no way of knowing where the original key was, but the most obvious answer was that the thieves had taken it with them.

As soon as the agents entered the room, the first thing they noticed was not chaos but the absence of the same. Usually when a robbery went down, the expectations were that there would be a damaged container of jewelry, brutally attacked safe or some other violent display but this time, it looked as if someone had easily taken out the diamonds from the safe.

Michael rushed forward and said, "It's all clean. It's as if the diamonds were just picked up from an open display box."

Jefferson looked up sharply and said, "But I thought that in order to open the case, David's thumbprint was required."

"Exactly!" exclaimed the victim "Now do you see why I am so distressed? They even had my thumbprint and they managed to evade the security without even raising a single alarm!"

So far, no one had looked into the safe, what mattered was that it was open and that it was empty, but now Agent Jefferson looked, and he felt an emotion that he had not felt in a long time – a complex composition of disbelief and surprise. The extent of the shock was such that he froze, for the first time in his life, Agent Jefferson Brown, the best of the best, froze in the face of evidence. This reaction on Jefferson's part was completely justified. There are a few objects in everyone's lives that force old memories to resurface, these memories may be good or bad, but when they resurface, they have a tremendous emotional as well as mental impact on the person and that was exactly what Jefferson was suffering from, *because the case contained two interlaced silver rings of unequal sizes.*

Seeing the odd manner Jefferson was behaving in, Sam and Michael peeked into the case, and they recognized the symbol immediately. This was not at all surprising, considering that the case had caused quite a stir in the FBI and was forever associated with Agent Jefferson's name.

Michael said, "That is *their* symbol, but I thought they were apprehended."

"They were," said Sam "This is impossible."

"No," said Jefferson in a grave tone "we are dealing with a copycat, and by the work done so far he is at least as good as the originals, if not better."

David was looking from one agent to another, and his mind was trying to make sense of the audio stimulus he was receiving, but so far, he was in the dark.

Finally, David said, "What are you talking about? You know who did this?"

"No, we don't," said Jefferson

"But you recognize the rings, don't you?"

"That is another matter," said Jefferson. His manner had changed from one of disbelief to one of attention and quick response. He could feel the adrenaline pumping through his veins while memories flashed in his mind.

After a moment he said, "Right, there is no use staying here any longer. I think we should check the footage once again and try to determine how the thief came in."

Michael and Sam responded with energy and enthusiasm and within minutes, the officers along with the owner of the estate, were in the security control room. The tape was being played right in front of three pairs of trained eyes and yet, no one was able to make a breakthrough.

Suddenly Michael said, "Stop it, seeing a recording that is clearly looped will not help us in any way, we are just wasting our time, what we need to do is think. How could a person gain access to the room long enough to gain root access to the system?"

Sam grunted and said, "Only if it were that easy, without CCTV and without any witnesses, we have no way of knowing how the robbery was committed."

Jefferson turned to David and said, "Are you sure the security staff did not see anything?"

David shook his head. "Like I said, there was no witness other than the guard outside the room where the diamonds were kept, and he is clearly in no condition to tell us anything."

"What about the guard you hired recently? for covering the cameras and keeping an eye on the security during the shift change. Is he positive that nothing was amiss?" asked

Michael.

"Well… I didn't ask him directly."

"Why not?"

"Because I was too distressed! Wait, I'll just call him." Saying this, David took his phone out of his pocket and calling his head of security, he said, "Send over the new guard."

After a moment, his expression morphed into one of surprise, "What?" he exclaimed. David hung up the call immediately and said, "I just found out who did it."

"Who?" asked Sam.

"The new guard, Dick. He hasn't shown up today."

Jefferson sighed and running over a hand on his forehead, he said, "It's always an inside man!"

Now David was furious, he said, "I should have seen this from the very beginning, the man was rude, arrogant and snubbed everyone."

Michael snapped at the sudden display of temper and said, "Look sir, all we can do now is try and catch him, that is if he is really guilty. It won't do us much good to speak ill of someone while the responsible party get away."

Sam nodded. "Yeah, I'll alert the police and send a unit over to his house, we'll get him soon enough."

While Sam headed out, Michael turned to Jefferson and said, "Even if we get the guard, any smart thief will make sure to at least get the diamonds out of the city ASAP if not out of the country. We need to alert the airports and the docks; those are the fastest and the most convenient."

Agent Jefferson nodded, and Michael headed out of the room as he dialed a number on his mobile. Now Jefferson was left alone with David in the room. The latter was pacing the length of the room frantically and wringing his hands. Jefferson could not help but think what a horrible time the man must be having.

"David, you need to calm down, we'll get them back," said Jefferson, in an attempt to ease the businessman.

David walked up to Jefferson and said, "You know what the diamonds meant for me Jefferson, their value was higher than any other set of diamonds I know of."

"I would have thought their emotional value was of more concern to you."

"Of course, that is a concern, but emotions cause emotional damage, but money causes financial damage, and you know as well as I do, that in today's world money is everything."

The blunt way in which David expressed his feelings somewhat disturbed Jefferson but he remained quiet. The man was in shock, and that was usually a time when they forgot to keep up appearance and just for a short interval of time, their true nature was revealed.

Sam walked into the room and said, "A unit is headed over to Dick's house as we speak."

"And I have alerted the airport and docks," said Michael, walking in. "I think we should talk to your head of security, someone might have noticed if Dick were up to something, we would have a better chance of making him talk if we knew exactly what he did and how he did it."

Agent Jefferson nodded. "That's correct, David Call him in, we'll meet him in the living room."

A few minutes later a very worried looking man was sitting in front of three FBI agents and the situation was doing nothing to ease his nerves. Whenever a crime is committed, the first thought that occupies the mind of an innocent is *what if the police suspected me?* This thought compels the imagination of the person to think of certain far-fetched and horrible scenarios that have an exceptionally low chance of occurring but seem to be quite possible to the nervous wreck of a man. Simon, the head of Security, was also thinking about what would happen if he were arrested or interrogated in a manner which was portrayed in spy movies, what if they tortured him for a nonexistent confession and in the end, he was forced to admit to doing something which he did not?

Such thoughts were making Simon's body react in a most inconvenient manner, firstly, he was sweating five times than he normally did, his heart rate was elevated, and his pupils were dilated. Although he tried to appear professional and mature, he was trembling from the inside like a five-year-old child who had been made to stand in front of a dangerous carnivore.

Jefferson said, "Mr. Simon, I understand that this is a most inconvenient situation and that you might be distressed or..."

Simon cut in and said, "Distressed? Who? Me? Oh no! I'm a professional sir. I'm not scared... I mean distressed! If anything, I am motivated to catch the man who slipped through my fingers."

Jefferson nodded and said, "I see. Would you please tell us if you noticed anything odd about Dick's behavior recently?"

"Recently?" scoffed Simon "The guy was a rude and arrogant animal, did not know how to talk politely, did not know how to behave with his superiors and mostly he irritated his coworkers and seemed to be against social contact of any sort."

Michael and Sam looked at each other. This was the result of the standard FBI training both had undergone. The personality traits which the man had mentioned were found in more than sixty percent of the common criminals.

But the problem was that this was not a common job, anyone pulling off a heist of this magnitude would try their best not to attract any unwanted attention, but Dick had clearly failed to do so.

"Did he show any signs of nervousness yesterday? Or did he do anything which might seem inappropriate?" asked Jefferson.

"Nothing more inappropriate than his usual behavior."

After asking a few more questions, and receiving a few more fruitless answers, the senior FBI agent allowed Simon to leave.

While leaving Simon turned, and in a most ordinary manner, he asked, "I am not a suspect, am I?"

Jefferson looked at him and said, "I cannot answer that."

With his expectation for a comforting answer crushed, Simon departed with his head full of dark torcher chambers and false confessions.

When he had left, Jefferson was about to say something when suddenly, Sam's phone rang, he had just placed it next to his ear when his expression changed to one of surprise. Without a word, he disconnected the call and then looked at Jefferson and Michael.

"What happened?" asked Michael.

"That was a call from the unit trying to locate Dick," replied Sam.

"And?" Jefferson prompted.

"And they found him. He has been hospitalized since early yesterday morning."

CHAPTER FOUR

"What?" exclaimed Jefferson. The piece of news that Dick had been in the hospital since the morning of the previous day had different effects on the inhabitants of the room. David was looking towards Sam as though he felt that the agent was lying, Sam's eyes were wide and he had wiped his forehead, a gesture which highlighted the fact that he was baffled, while Jefferson had just exclaimed and was staring at the mobile in Sam's hand as if he felt certain that the harmless piece of technology was playing a joke on him. Michael looked surprised, but after a few moments he fell into deep thought.

"How is this possible?" asked David.

Jefferson looked at Sam who stared back at him blankly. Suddenly all heads turned towards Michael as he said, "It is not impossible, just very, very hard, even with a lot of planning."

"What do you mean? Cloning?" asked Sam.

Michael laughed a little and said, "Nothing of that sort, this is not a science fiction movie. The thing is the thieves are smart, this proves it. The staff says that they saw Dick *on duty,* but the hospital record confirms that he was admitted when he claims he was."

Jefferson grew impatient, he said, "Yes, we know that. What is your point?"

"My point is that there is only one way they could have managed to pull off the heist and that was with the help of an inside man and now we know who that was."

"And that man is Dick?" suggested Sam

Michael shook his head and said, "Not quite. It was an entirely different man altogether, a stranger, a man who was impersonating Dick with such perfection that no one even realized that a substitution had taken place. It was all an act, a well-planned and elaborate scheme executed with perfection."

Jefferson shook his head. "That is a far-fetched theory. It is not possible to impersonate a man with such perfection. Even if they could, there is absolutely no way they could have done it in less than a week. They had to monitor his behavior, the way he spoke, everything, and that too when Dick spent most of his time here, on duty, which meant they could not monitor his activities."

Michael said, "It's far-fetched, I agree, but it is the only logical explanation, because quite frankly, I don't believe that Dick has got some twin brother who has managed to evade detection since the time he was born."

Sam snickered. "Well, it appears we are going to have to wait for the man himself to wake up to shed some more light on the matter."

"What happened to him anyway? Poison?" asked Jefferson.

"Nope, a blow on the head which resulted in a serious concussion," replied Sam. "His family says that he was on his way to work in the morning when he was allegedly kidnapped for a short duration of time. No one saw him, a while later the family received a call from a stranger saying that he had found the man in an alley."

"Did they file a police report?" asked Michael.

Sam shook his head, "Nope. They say they were too worried about Dick's health to do anything else at that time."

Jefferson stood up and said, "All right, David, there is nothing more to be done here. A team will scour the crime scene for any evidence left behind by the thieves and we will keep you updated about the progress."

David nodded and the agents took their leave. Once in the car, all three of them began following different threads of thought which had varied beginnings but the same conclusion. The conclusion was a question, *how had they done it?* Usually when a robbery is committed, the method is known and the guilty party must be found and brought to justice, but in this case, the way in which the robbery was committed was as much of a riddle as who had committed it.

Jefferson did not say even a single word during the return journey and the younger agents were wise enough to realize that it was best not to disturb him.

Upon reaching their destination, Jefferson went into the office and shut the door. As far as he could remember there had never been a case that he had taken personally, he believed that an objective view was the best when approaching a case as that enabled a person to form theories devoid of their opinion, however, this case was different. This time there was someone out there who had targeted Jefferson, the person had taunted him and then committed a robbery under his very nose. To say the least, this experience was highly humiliating. But Jefferson was not one of the people who let their emotions hinder their performance, he had complete control over his emotions and that was a quality which was particularly useful in the present situation.

While any other person would have been infuriated and many of them would have felt like smashing things, Jefferson took the situation as a challenge and thus, instead of getting demoralized, he was motivated. With the intention of refreshing his memory on the details of the case of the original thieves he decided to dig into the case file. As he turned the pages of the file, various instances began going through his mind and soon he was lost in memories of the past.

After a while he closed the file and devoted his mind entirely to his thoughts. He was trying to figure out how to get an upper hand against the thieves. His mind was formulating various situations when there was a knock on his door and Sam entered, along with Michael.

Sam was practically jumping with excitement. His eyes were wide and after a long time, Jefferson saw that Michael's facial expression was one of excitement as well.

Jefferson said, "What has gotten into you two? What did you find?"

Sam placed a laptop on Jefferson's desk and showing him a dark footage, he said, "Look. Just look at the footage, and you will see."

Everyone focused on the display screen of the laptop, for over a minute all they could see were dark shapes moving around, then there was a small light towards the end of the screen and a moment later, the footage ended.

Jefferson looked at Sam as though the young agent had just pulled a stupid prank on him. "Please tell me what you expected me to see here."

"Nothing," said Sam.

"Nothing?" asked Jefferson.

Michael said, "Yes, nothing, but look what happens when you enhance the Image...show him, Sam."

Sam pulled up the edited footage and this time, towards the end of the footage, just for a split second, there was a car visible. With its license plate.

Jefferson's eyes went wide and now, he was sharing the excitement which had infected Sam and Michael when they had entered the office. He zoomed the image and then took a long look at it, finally he said, "Did you check out the records yet?"

"Yep!" replied Sam with a flourish "The car was bought quite some time ago, registered to a shell corporation, but there is an address we could check."

"Very well, you two go and check it out. Remember, do not engage, just survey and report back. If we get something, we do not want to alert them," cautioned Jefferson.

"Survey? I think we have enough to bring them in and question them till they break," said Michael.

"No, we need to get the diamonds back and find out if he has any co-conspirators. A guy clever enough to pull off a heist with such sophistication is someone we need to exercise caution with."

Sam nodded reluctantly and both agents headed out of the office. Michael excused himself to go to the washroom while Sam offered to get the car out front and meet him outside. Michael went into the washroom and walked up to the basin, he splashed some water on his face and tried to relax. Just as he was doing this another agent entered the washroom and began washing his hands. Now Michael grew uncomfortable. Ever since he had left alcohol he had been suffering from certain uncomfortable symptoms, one of them was a feeling of sudden anxiety and a strong craving for alcohol. At the time of these episodes, Michael had to focus in order to stay true to the promise that he had made to Jefferson. He was having one of those episodes now, he washed his face again and could feel his hands shaking slightly.

"Are you all right?" asked the other agent in the washroom.

"Yes, I'm fine," replied Michael.

He splashed some more water on his face and looked at himself in the mirror. He stared straight into his own eyes and after a moment, he had regained control over his body and mind. He wiped his hands and headed out of the washroom, straight towards where Sam was waiting for him in the car.

As Michael Entered the car, Sam looked at his face and said, "Are you feeling all right Michael? You look pale."

"It's nothing, just tired," said Michael.

This answer did not seem to satisfy Sam, but he decided not to ask any more questions. The reason for this decision of his was that he had seen that Michael's hands had a slight tremor. Few people knew Sam had an elder brother who was an alcoholic. Sam had spent years praying to God that Alcohol would go extinct from Earth but then he had grown up and realized that the problem was not with the world, it was his brother who was to be blamed. He recognized the symptoms of withdrawal very well and now he knew what Michael was going through. For a moment he decided to keep aside his dislike for the man and try to help him combat the craving for the bottle.

Sam said, "So what do you think?"

"About what?"

"About the case, about how they committed the robbery."

"I already explained my theory today," said Michael.

"Come on, you must have a better one by now!"

"Unfortunately, I am fresh out of new theories," admitted Michael. "The only one that I have is the one that I explained to you and Jefferson in the morning."

Sam sighed and said, "Well, I don't know, but I think that there must be a more probable explanation, one that is not so fantastical."

Michael looked at Sam for a moment and then said, "Thank You, Sam."

Sam looked at him sharply and said, "For what?"

"Nothing, I just wanted to thank you and I wanted to assure you that I know."

"Know what?"

Michael stared at the road ahead and said, "To attain the luster of gold, one must withstand the ferocious heat."

Sam said, "That is a good one, who said that?"

"It's an original," stated Michael.

"Well done, then."

After a rather impatient wait, Sam eased the car to a halt. They had reached the building where Rafool Edmunds lived, at least according to the records. To put it mildly, this was not one of the best neighborhoods in New York.

Both Michael and Sam sat where they were, unsure of how to proceed. Sam asked, "How do you want to do this?"

"I would have preferred a direct confrontation, but that appears to be out of the question."

"Jefferson just ordered that we had to survey, I don't think he even thought of how we would do that," replied Sam

"That means he trusted us to find a way."

Sam said, "Let's go and ring his bell, I'll say we are looking into a missing persons case."

"He is cunning enough to rob diamonds without leaving a trace, you think he won't make that connection?" asked

Michael.

Sharing his just cropped-up idea Michael said, "Sam, give me the number for his house."

"Why? What are you going to do?" asked Sam.

"Spook him," replied Michael "I am going to say that a damaged vehicle was found with papers on his name present in the dashboard."

"And that would make him nervous, so he would go to check on the car, wherever he had hidden it, right?" asked Sam.

"Correct," said Michael.

A moment later, both the agents had their ears close to Michael's mobile. The line kept ringing, but no one picked up, they tried again, but met with the same response.

Finally, Michael disconnected the phone and said, "This can mean only one thing."

"That he is not at home," concluded Sam.

"Well, I think of this as an opportunity," said Michael.

"If you are thinking what I think you are thinking, then it is a very bad idea."

Precisely three minutes later, Michael had convinced Sam that it was the best idea to "gain access" to Rafool's apartment while he was out. Although Sam had pointed out that Michael's plan felt more like a B&E rather than an investigation, but he had ultimately agreed. Now, Sam was on his way up to the apartment while, Michael was keeping an eye on the building in case Rafool returned. Sam had managed to get an image of the man from the DMR database, and their target was revealed to be a heavily bearded man with droopy eyes and a balding head. Michael concluded from the man's looks that he was the kind of person who would spend the better part of his life sitting on a couch in front of the TV and he was sure that Sam would be able to handle the guy even if there was a confrontation.

The sky was starting to get darker and just a few moments later raindrops began falling on the car's windshield. Michael was getting more impatient with each passing moment. With the intention of trying to calm himself, he looked out of the window, and he saw an old man sitting on the sidewalk. The man just nodded his head as a woman walked by him and placed a small packet near him, then, after a moment, the man opened the packet, took out a sandwich wrapped in foil and began eating it. Seeing such a gesture on the part of the woman, a smile spread on Michael's face. But then the woman attracted his attention, she was going into the building where the apartment was located. Michael's first instinct was to warn Sam, but then he thought that if he went warning Sam at the sight of every person that passed by, Sam's entire time would be spent answering the phone. Michael picked up Rafool's photo once again and began scrutinizing it. There was something odd...something unusual about the image, but Michael could not figure out what. It felt like what he was seeing was wrong, but he could not understand why. He was trying to find the answer to his question when suddenly his phone rang, the caller ID confirmed that the call was from Sam.

Michael picked up the phone immediately and said, "Sam! What's up?"

"Come up here, right now!" said Sam in a hoarse and urgent voice.

"What?" asked Michael disbelievingly "But what if someone shows up?"

"No one's coming, this thing is way more complicated than we thought."

Sam's tone was enough to tell Michael that the matter was serious, he ran out of the car and went up the building. He saw that the door of Rafool's apartment was open and when he went inside, a cold shiver went down his spine.

Sam was standing in the middle of the living room, the house was scantily furnished, and it was clear that there had been no human inhabitants within its four walls for quite some time. There was a small table in the very center of the room, on this table was a white envelope. But that was not the eerie part. The most disturbing thing in the room was what was on the wall – the name, Rafool Edmunds, written in blood.

CHAPTER FIVE

For a moment Michael could not process what he was seeing, because he felt as though he was in one of the horror movies that made one lay awake at night. His mind was suddenly wide awake and aware of every element of his surroundings. He was aware of the damp and cold room, he was aware of Sam standing right next to him and staring at him, assessing his reaction, and he was aware of the writing on the wall, which made much more sense now that he was looking at it closely. The name Rafool Edmunds was written in block letters and the last three letters of the first name and first two letters of the last name were underlined together so that they read as - ...fool Ed...

Fooled. That was what was spelled, and Michael realized with a start that all of it had been a deception, a setup, that the thief had let them see the number plate intentionally. He had guessed that they would follow the lead and end up in this house, right where he wanted them. Instinctively, Michael took a defensive position, the idea that he was where the thief wanted him sent a rush of adrenaline through a system, and his mind automatically activated the defensive mode of his body. Michael was ready for anything to happen, but nothing did. After a moment, he relaxed.

Sam, who was staring at him, said, "You know what? I am ninety per cent certain that I had the exact same reaction when I'd seen this."

"You realize what this means, don't you?" asked Michael.

"Yes, I do. We played right into the guy's hands."

"Did you call Jefferson yet?"

"He's on his way. Let's not touch anything."

The agents did not have to wait long. Jefferson was on site within fifteen minutes, with backup, and his reaction was similar to Sam and Michael's, but the only difference was that Jefferson's eyes were a clear indication of how angry he was. It was quite natural, after what he had been through anyone would have been angry, but then he saw the envelope on the table. The anger left his eyes, and its place was taken by intrigue. Everyone watched anxiously as Jefferson walked up to the table and picked up the envelope. Jefferson's name was typed in bold across the middle of the envelope and inside it there was a single piece of paper. Jefferson read it and Michael saw that his back tensed, he saw as Jefferson delicately placed the paper back in the envelope. It was evident that he was fighting the urge to crumple the paper and stomp on it.

Michael wanted to ask what was written on the piece of paper, but he did not say anything. He was sure that Sam shared the same curiosity as himself but the look that Jefferson gave them was clear – *not now, not here.*

"Sam, we need to interview the other occupants of the floor, someone must have definitely seen something," said Jefferson.

Sam said, "Judging by the amount of planning which the guy has evidently put into this job, I'd say that's a long shot, but still, I'll check with the occupants."

"That would be quite a list," said Michael.

Michael was entirely correct in his observation. The building was divided into several large floors and the houses located in these floors were far from spacious. It appeared that the builder had tried to cram in as many apartments as possible on a single floor and thus, the number of occupants was a little higher than average.

Jefferson beckoned Michael and Sam, and both the agents followed him out with puzzled expressions on their faces. Once they were standing outside the building, Jefferson said, "This guy is smart..."

"Oh, we believe you!" cut in Sam.

Jefferson rolled his eyes and said, "Let me complete. As I was saying, this guy is smart, and he knows that. This combination almost always results in a certain degree of overconfidence and that is what he is displaying now."

"What do you mean?" asked Michael.

In answer, Jefferson handed Michael the envelope which he had picked up from the table in the house. Inside was a single piece of paper with two lines printed across it. After reading the two lines both the young agents felt a sense of excitement and tension.

"He's done it again," said Jefferson, voicing the thought which was in the mind of both the men standing in front of him.

Indeed, he had done it again. The chit of paper was an indication of where the thief was going to commit his next robbery, it was the house of a very wealthy business tycoon, Harold Williamson. But there was only one problem, according to the chit, the thief had claimed that he would rob "the exquisite items" from the businessman's personal collection, he had even mentioned a date, ten days later. However, as far as anyone knew, the businessman did not have any personal collection, all that he was interested in was running his company and playing golf, he had no other hobby and did not need one.

Michael said, "Will you warn him too?"

"I'm obligated to," replied Jefferson.

Sam was about to say something when his mobile rang. After listening to the speaker on the other end for a few seconds and contributing a few words to the conversation, Sam hung up.

It was with an expression of urgency that he said, "We need to get to the hospital, the guard, Dick, the doctors say he is fit enough to talk to us."

No one wasted any time. They were sitting in the car within seconds and Jefferson expertly weaved through the traffic to get them to the hospital in the most efficient time possible. Once they were at the hospital, they were met by a senior doctor who briefed them about Dick's health situation. The doctor claimed that although Dick had been injured, the blows were expertly landed to make sure that there was only temporary suffering with no lasting effects. From the medical point of view Dick was in an exceptionally good condition for someone who had been abducted, and the doctor was sure the man had not even suffered any trauma. That was the condition of the patient from the physical point of view, but the condition was quite different from the psychological point of view. The man was angry, confused and did not know who to blame for his unpleasant experience. As a result, Dick was being extremely rude to the hospital staff and doctors. Jefferson listened to all of this with a straight face. While he was paying attention to what the doctor was telling them, he was impatient to talk to the man. Finally, they were led into Dick's room. They were greeted by the image of a man of a large build propped up on the bed with an irritable look on his face. The man was in his mid-forties and had a scraggly beard.

Dick looked up and said, "Who're you?"

Jefferson stepped forward and said, "Hello Mr. Smith, my name is Jefferson Brown, I'm an FBI special agent."

Dick's cheeks turned red as he said, "I'll tell you what you are! You are late! I was abducted, do you understand? ABDUCTED!"

"Calm down, Dick," said the doctor.

"Calm down? they failed to protect a citizen!" said Dick in an accusing manner.

"I would be interested to see your reaction when we tell you that we are here to interrogate a *suspect*," said Jefferson.

Now Dick's anger subsided. He said, "What do you mean? What have I done?"

"Did you know that your employer was in possession of a very valuable set of diamonds?" asked Jefferson.

Dick scoffed and said, "Yeah, diamonds with a fancy French name, so what?"

"They've been stolen."

Dick had a genuine look of surprise on his face when he said, "And you suspect me? I was in a hospital!"

"And yet we have you on camera and we even have eyewitnesses who saw you on the property on which the crime was committed," said Jefferson.

"And when was this crime committed?"

"On the day you were allegedly kidnapped."

"Are you even hearing what you are saying? First, you say that I was at the property, now you say that I was kidnapped, I believe you are the one who needs a doctor. A mental one."

As serious as the topic was, Michael had to stifle his laugh. To Michael, the idea of Jefferson consulting a "mental doctor" was a very funny one, so much so, that he could not control himself.

Dick looked at him and said, "Did I just make a joke?"

Michael was instantly ready with a witty comeback, he said, "It's your feeble attempt to conceal your guilt that is making me laugh."

Sam looked at him and raised an eyebrow. Jefferson said, "Why should we believe that you are innocent? You could be a coconspirator."

"I could be, but I am not. Look, there must be video footage of the hospital that shows my admittance and even the doctors saw me!"

"Like I said, we also have that kind of proof, you will need to do better than that," said Jefferson.

Now, Dick was losing his cool once again. "I would never do something that would smear my reputation in the security business, especially not when someone had asked for me. It is my job, the only one that I have, it's my kid's future we are talking about!"

Jefferson cut in and said, "Wait, what did you just say? asked for you? What do you mean?"

"I mean that my boss told me that the employers had specifically asked for my services for this job," replied Dick.

Jefferson was about to say something when Michael cut in and said, "Why would they do that?"

"They said I had worked for some friend of theirs and they were pretty satisfied with my work."

"And had you?" asked Jefferson.

"Had I what?"

"Had you worked for a friend of theirs?"

"I have worked for a lot of people; I don't remember their family trees or their list of friends! I just took it as an opportunity."

Jefferson was about to say something when he was interrupted again, this time by Sam, "How did your boss get to know this? Did someone come over to meet him or did he go to meet Mr. David?”

“No, they just called and said they needed another guard, the boss told me that just after he had hung up, the man called again and asked for me specifically. The boss was incredibly happy with me, said I’d done the firm proud and all that.”

Sam did not say anything, but his eyes were enough to tell anyone that he had figured out something important. When he did not say anything else for a moment, Jefferson said, “Who was this man?”

“I don’t know, just some man,” replied Dick.

Jefferson got up and said, “We’ll be in touch, Mr. Smith.”

Saying this, the agents exited the hospital room.

Jefferson ran a hand through his hair and said, “Well, now we need to know who this man was, let’s go talk to his boss.”

“No need,” said Michael “I think I know who it was.”

“How do you know?” asked Jefferson.

“I just do. It’s a perfectly logical assumption. I’ll fill you in on the way to the David Wood’s place.”

“Why do we need to go there again? It takes too much time,” said Sam.

“Trust me, it’ll be worth it,” replied Michael.

The agents soon reached the car and were on their way to the residence of David Wood in no time. Sam and Michael utilized the time of the journey to explain their theories to Jefferson.

Michael went first and said, “Whenever someone needs to hire security, they contact a security firm, that is routine for middle-class people, not billionaires, they have someone else do it for them. That someone varies from job to job but when the security is concerned the logical choice is the head of security.”

Jefferson nodded his head and said, "Simon."

"Precisely."

Now it was Sam's turn to explain, he said, "But I doubt he is guilty."

"What do you mean?" asked Jefferson.

"Look, there are two things which pointed me in the right direction, there were *two calls*, and it was in the second one that the man, asked for Dick specifically. Nowadays, all phones have an electronic chip in them, which means that they are digitalized to some extent, and thus, they are hackable. If I timed it right, I would be able to hack into the phone to trick the receiver of the call into thinking that the call was from someone else, in this case, Simon. To make my voice sound authentic, I could take any approach, from voice transformation software to changing the voice without any assistance of technology."

Jefferson said, "So basically what you are saying is that while Simon thought that the security agency had just allotted a random guy to them, the thieves made sure that the agency sent over the person they wanted for the job."

"Exactly! Now we only have to find out why they chose this specific man."

After a moment, Jefferson spoke up. "I know the answer to that," he said. "Previously we were under the impression that the thieves only had a week to plan the heist, as Dick had only been at the job for a week."

"So?"

"So don't you see, they wanted to have Dick as they had been studying him, they had been scrutinizing his behavior, the way he talked, the way he moved so that when the time came one of them would be prepared to pass as the guard. And as to why they chose him, the answer is obvious, the man is an easy mark. He has an unpleasant nature, so no one talks to him much, which reduces the chance of the deception failing, and then his physical appearance is also easily achievable, full beard and heavy build. Anyone could do it. Our original assumption was wrong, they didn't have just a week, they took their time to perfect their plan."

Sam and Michael were listening closely to what Jefferson had been saying, now Sam leant forward and said, "And here we were thinking that the chubby guy in a hospital room was the mastermind behind the robbery."

CHAPTER SIX

Two men were sitting in a café. Their personalities were in such contrast that it was hard to imagine that they were acquainted with each other. One of the men was tall and tough with a fit body and a clean-shaven face, while the other was of a humble physique but was the possessor of some strength nonetheless, there were large spectacles on his eyes, and he had a full black beard which appeared quite rough, like his hair.

These two men were not friends. Far from it. But their association was quite atypical, they were not fond of each other, at all. The man with the beard knew everything about the clean-shaven guy, but the ripped one had only a few pieces of information about the man who was seated in front of him. Both of them needed the assistance of the other and this circumstance resulted in an uncomfortable air around the men.

The tall man, Calvin Hughes, said, "There is no going back now, are you sure about the plan?"

"Yes, I am and do not ask me that question again," replied Oliver with a pronounced British accent.

"Fine! I'm just saying," replied Calvin "So the next step is to further communicate, correct?"

"Yes, how do you suggest we do that?" asked Oliver.

"Same as before?"

"No, they will be alert this time, we take no risks."

"Then how?"

Oliver was silent. A minute passed, then two, finally he said, "I have an idea, it's quite simple, I'll just need my computer."

Calvin nodded as if he understood, then withdrawing an envelope from his bag, he said, "This is everything you asked for."

Oliver took the envelope from Calvin's hand and examined its contents with a smile. Till now, everything was going according to plan and his plan was not simple nor was it humble. They had stolen *Les morceaux de lumière*, and that was just the beginning.

CHAPTER SEVEN

It was evening and Michael was sitting alone in his apartment. The television was switched on, but his mind was elsewhere. In his mind, he was replaying moments from earlier in the day. He remembered how the three of them had reached David's house and asked Simon if he had called to request for Dick's services but, as they had suspected, the man was completely unaware of what had happened. Jefferson had informed the owner of their theory as to how the crime had been committed and in response, David had spoken the original line which was spoken by every victim of theft – *"I want my property back!"* Sam had proceeded to inform the businessman that they were very well aware of his desire, even though it was quite "unusual". This remark seemed to have snubbed David, as he had cut short the conversation.

Michael stood up and went over to a side table, on this table a tray was placed with a bottle of alcohol and beside it was a bottle of water. Michael walked up to the table and took the bottle of water. He looked at the other bottle once, just once, and then turned his back away. His throat felt parched as he poured himself a glass of water and drained it. There were various aspects to the case which were quite unusual, that might stick out. He tried to make some connection between these points but was unable to do so, nothing came up that might point him in the right direction. He picked up his mobile from the side table and decided to call his sister, Mary, she always succeeded in lifting his spirits.

Mary received the call on the third ring. "Hello Michael, what's up?"

"Did you watch the news?"

"Yes, I did, I suppose you are working on the case."

"I am."

"Found any leads yet?"

"Yes, but they just seem to confirm that the thief is quite smart."

"Don't praise him too much. Everyone can make mistakes if they are not careful, and that means you need to be alert and look out for the mistakes."

"I feel as though this is too much for me."

"Don't you dare doubt my brother, I know him better than anyone, nothing is too much for him."

Michael smiled. "Thanks, sis."

"Anytime, bro. Now, I need to go, have some business to attend to."

"What sort of business?"

"Some clients say that they are not satisfied with the products"

"Tell them they dare not doubt my sister. She's the best at everything she does."

"Thanks bro."

Michael smiled and said, "Anytime, sis."

After Michael had hung up, he continued to stare at the television and did not even realize when he fell asleep. Unfortunately, he was jolted awake only two minutes later as his phone buzzed. There was a text message from an unidentified number, instructing him to open his door. Puzzled but quite fearless, Michael got up and opened his front door. He was ready for any situation, or so he thought, as he was taken aback when he opened the door. There was no one at the door, rather, there was a small package on the doorstep. Michael picked it up gingerly and went back in. He carefully placed the package on the table and decided to inspect it. He was an FBI agent, and always being on the alert was an occupational necessity. After forty minutes of rigorous inspection which involved prodding the package with a long stick and even tapping it with a small hammer, Michael concluded that it was safe to finally satisfy his curiosity as to what was contained within it. He opened the package and inside was a small wooden box, and within the box was something that puzzled Michael even more. Within the box, there was a single chit of paper and on this chit, two words were printed in bold – *Hello Michael*.

(II)

Sam was sitting in a bar. His fingers were curled around a glass of chilled beer, but he was uncomfortable while drinking it. There are times when we do not realize the risks of some actions or the depth of certain problems until we have seen someone else suffer from the consequences, and that was exactly what was happening to Sam. He had always been aware of Michael's case, but now that he was working with him and was able to see how miserable he was, he looked at the glass of alcohol in his hand in an apprehensive way. Finally, he decided not to drink, it was easier than spending the entire night awake, pondering the question – *was he in control?*

He got up and exited the bar. A little shiver went down his spine, but he attributed it to the events of the day so far. He had been involved in active investigations before, but this was different, their opponents were bolder and apparently, smarter than the ones he had encountered in the past. As he got into a cab, Sam could not help but think what the thieves would be doing at the moment, planning, perhaps. After all, they knew they had one of the best agents on their track, one mistake from their side could result in a catastrophe for them. He tried to think what Jefferson would do next, he had told them that he was going to inform Harold Williamson, but Sam felt that he had something else on his mind.

Sam was soon standing outside the door of his own apartment. Upon opening the door, he froze. It was dark, and it was not supposed to be dark. With great courage he switched on the flashlight of his mobile and stepped in. He switched on the light and let out a sigh of relief. He looked up at the bulb which he always left on when leaving his house. The switch was on, but the bulb was not emitting any light. Sam sighed again and shook his head. No one other than his parents knew that he was afraid of the dark and that the intensity of his fear was just a notch below what most people would call a phobia. It had never gotten in the way of a case, yet, but Sam was sure that it was just a matter of time when he would have to either face his fear or compromise a case. He took a deep breath and switched off the light once again. Everything was fine for two seconds. Then Sam's heart rate elevated, and his hands went cold, he was on the verge of starting hyperventilating when he switched on the light again. *I will do it some other time,* thought Sam, *not today, not today...*

(III)

Jefferson was sitting alone in his living room. His wife was in the kitchen and their daughter, Penny, was drawing in her room. A few years ago, his wife had made him start meditating. She had said it was good for him, as the cases he was working on had too much impact on his day-to-day life.

Little did she know that even while meditating Jefferson thought about the cases. His wife was constantly worrying about his health, and that meant she was constantly lecturing him about how he should not be working all the time. Jefferson knew that he should listen to what she said, but he just couldn't get his mind to shift focus from the cases, especially not from the one he was currently investigating. Today, an idea had crept into his mind. An idea which, if executed, could either give them a serious advantage over the thieves or it could be disastrous. Jefferson was not the man who would doubt himself. He knew what was right and what was wrong, but this time he had no idea if he was right or wrong.

The only other person in his life whom he considered to be in possession of a perfect moral compass was his wife. She was one of the people who had been gifted with the ability to guide the ones who were lost. Now, he was waiting for his wife to join him to discuss the matter with her. Ten minutes passed, fifteen and then twenty. Just as Jefferson was about to get up, his wife entered the living room. She sat down on the sofa beside him and gazed at the framed newspaper articles that were hung on the wall of the living room. They were the headlines of some of Jefferson's most famous cases. Jefferson's eyes went over each of the headlines and he realized, with delight, that he remembered each detail of all the cases perfectly. Martha was also smiling, although her smile had a different reason altogether. She was a journalist, and it was with immense pride that she wrote about the successful career of her husband. While it was true that she was the author of some of the articles on the wall, she was not one of the people who exaggerated the facts, even for someone they loved. While she was writing, Martha was just a journalist, nothing more, but nothing less than the best. In fact, her passion for her career was one of the things that had attracted Jefferson to her and till this day, he admired this quality of his wife.

Jefferson said, "Martha, I need your opinion on something."

"Work related or related to what you're going to wear to Penny's annual function?" asked Martha with a smile.

"It's work," said Jefferson without a smile.

Martha sensed the gravity of the situation instantly. She knew when her husband was troubled. "What is it?"

"I have a case, there has been a robbery at David Wood's place, as you might know."

"*Might* know?" asked Martha with disbelief "I wrote an article on that myself, the thief is quite skilled."

Jefferson nodded and said, "Yes, but there is something else, today the thief staged a scene for us, a false lead."

"You mean that apartment where the FBI has sent a team?"

"How did you know about that?" asked Jefferson with a raised eyebrow.

"I have my sources. But I never knew that it was the thief who had sent you there."

Jefferson looked at his wife and said, "Martha there are some things, certain pieces of evidence that have not been made available to anyone, not even the media and to get your opinion, I will have to share those with you, but as you know, it will..."

"... be in complete confidence," completed Martha. "I know, you don't have to tell me that. I would never write about anything confidential that you share with me. When you share such things with me it is with the trust that I am your wife, and I will never even think of betraying that."

Jefferson gave his wife a grateful smile and took out his mobile. He showed Martha an image and the latter's eyes widened.

"But that's the sign left behind by the ring thieves!" exclaimed Martha.

"Correct, and I found it at the crime scene."

"So do you think it's copycat?" asked Martha "That would explain why he sent you the chit, telling you when the robbery would be committed, he wanted to get your attention."

"That's what I thought. But that is not all. Earlier today, at the flat, the thief had not just called us to humiliate us, he left a message for me."

"What message?"

In response, Jefferson showed his wife an image of the piece of paper which the thief had left behind for him. After inspecting the image for almost thirty seconds, Martha looked at her husband with a glint in her eyes.

She said, "This is good, he has made a mistake. Owing to his overconfidence, he has given you a chance to catch him."

"Be that as it may, I don't want to fail this time. The man has already made the bureau look bad twice, I cannot risk that happening again."

"So, what do you have in mind?" asked Martha with a puzzled expression on her face.

"That is what I wanted to talk to you about, I think I have found a way to make sure that we have an upper hand."

"And what is it?"

"I will get them out of prison," said Jefferson in a grave manner.

"Get who out of prison?"

"The thieves, the original ones."

An uncomfortable silence prevailed in the room after this statement. The reason behind this silence was not just the fact that Jefferson was talking about getting two cunning criminals out of prison, or that this might give them a chance to escape, it was more about how it *felt*. Jefferson had made a lot of effort to get the thieves behind bars and getting them out felt as though he was being forced to go against what he had worked so hard to achieve. Martha understood what her husband must be feeling, further, she was of a practical turn of mind and the second thought that came to her mind, after the concern for her husband, was what the negative effects of this step might be.

Martha gently laid a hand on her husband's arm and said, "Have you given it enough thought? I mean, there is some risk involved."

"Considerable risk," agreed Jefferson. "But we will be monitoring them at all times."

"But why would they do it? They hate you, that much is evident."

"Since my proposal has been approved on my guarantee that they will not escape my custody, I can offer them a deal for their services. Also, to them this whole thing is a game, the robberies, the risk, everything. They hate me because I won, but if I give them another chance, they will be more than willing to go all in."

"But in what way would they help you?" asked Martha.

"Well, the copycat thieves had the benefit of making the first move, they took their time to act, but we don't have enough time to think and react. As far as I can see, the only ones who can predict what they are planning or what their aim is, are the original ones. Further, it may have a psychological effect on the thieves which might be quite useful for us. You see, they idolize the ring thieves, and if they find out that they are the ones who have been pitted against them, they will suffer a setback, to say the least."

"They?" asked Martha.

"What?"

"You just referred to the thief you are after, but instead of singular, you used plural, why?"

"I said they because we're not sure of the gender."

"But you *meant* plural, it was evident from your tone. I understand you better than anyone."

Jefferson was silent. Without even realizing he had formed a theory and had unintentionally voiced it as well.

"I just think that it's not a one-man job," said Jefferson.

Martha nodded and was silent for a few moments. Then she said, "And is it necessary to get them both out of prison?"

Jefferson tried to keep himself in the shoes of the thieves to find the answer to Martha's question. Within an instant, the answer was obvious to him.

"Yes, it is. I would try my best to get only one of them out, but I don't think I would succeed. They will not help otherwise; they've always been an inseparable team."

Martha nodded her head in understanding. Had she faced this situation in the early years of their marriage, she would have been concerned, even troubled, by what her husband was proposing to do. But now, she knew better. She knew that she could always trust him and his ability to handle any situation.

She voiced what she felt perfectly as she said, "Do what you think is right. I trust you."

These were the very words that Jefferson needed to hear. He took a deep breath and took out his phone. He needed to make some calls, he needed to get two prisoners back into society.

CHAPTER EIGHT

Maximum Security Prison:

The next morning a man was sitting on his bed, in his cell. Silence surrounded him and there were two reasons for the same. The first was that it was quarter to four in the morning, and it was the time when most of the people were not highly active. The second reason was that the man was in a high-security prison, and he was alone in his cell. He had a book of crossword puzzles and a pencil in his hand. After a moment he took off his glasses, lay the book aside and stared into space. He was a middle-aged man with graying, black hair and a fit, although thin physique. His manner was one that made a strong statement that he was one of the people who preferred to use their brains rather than brawn.

The man got up and stretched. After some light exercise, he looked at the small watch at the corner of his bed. The time was four twenty. The man once again took up his book of crossword puzzles. Since as far as he could remember, had never been able to sleep after three in the Morning. There was no reason for this, it was just that his body clock was set in this way. This habit, although tiresome, was quite good for the profession he had chosen. A thief. One of the best, literally, as the only other thief, whom he referred to as one of the best, was his partner and thus, their team was *the best*. There was no competition. They had pulled off jobs that common thieves would hesitate to even think about. There was nothing that they could not have achieved together. They were the best in the game, but then a young FBI agent had come along and ruined it all.

The man, Brandon by name, was quite sure that the lawmen were nothing more than people who had the compulsive desire to be praised and be the hero, which was why they spent a large amount of the time of their lives trying to pull themselves higher by putting others behind bars. As these thoughts went across his mind, Brandon smirked and shook his head, these officers had no idea how exciting it was on the other side. Sure, there was more threat, but there was also freedom and thrill. As Brandon saw it, everyone was given a chance to improve the quality of the moment of their death while they were alive. They could either die thinking about their unfulfilled dreams and aspirations or they could think about how they had done everything they wanted to do and more. Brandon believed in trying to go for the latter option. While life had made sure that he could never fulfill his dream of becoming a painter, Brandon made sure that no matter what he did, he was going to live life to the fullest.

Finally, after the wait of what felt like an eternity, a guard slipped the day's newspaper through an opening in the gate of his cell. Brandon leapt up from bed and took up the paper just as a child snatches a chocolate, and as far as Brandon was concerned, the newspaper was no less than the chocolate. Usually nothing new took place, nothing new of criminal interest, to be more precise. Crimes were committed, but for the usual motives and in the same boring manner, but recently there had been a deviation from this trend. A robbery had been committed, and the thing that had been stolen was something that held a special place in Brandon's life. *Les morceaux de Lumiere*, the diamonds that had once been the target of Brandon and his partner, had been stolen. But it was not the beauty of the diamonds that made them special, it was the fact that it was during the attempt to steal these very diamonds that Brandon and his partner had been caught. Brandon got so engrossed in reading about the latest developments in the case that he did not realize how much time had passed. Finally, it was time for visitation, but this did not mean anything to Brandon. He never had any visitors, nor did he want any. He wanted to meet only one person in the world, but she was not coming to meet him, she could not. Brandon was so sure of her inability to come to meet him as he was certain that if she ever gained that ability, there would certainly be a mention of it in the papers.

Suddenly, the door to Brandon's cell opened and a guard entered. The guard, named Wiggins, was a huge man in his mid-forties, although his looks were menacing, he was one of the friendliest guards in the prison. He was strict but friendly, a rare combination. Brandon looked at him with a raised eyebrow, but Wiggins just beckoned him to get up. Brandon did not move. He never did anything until he knew what was going on.

Wiggins said, "Come on Brandon, you have a visitor."

Brandon did not move an inch. He said, "A visitor? For me?" He laughed. "Is it first April today?"

"I'm not joking, now get up and come out, I won't ask again."

Brandon got to his feet and walked over to the entrance of his cell. He was led towards a room in the prison which was usually used for the meetings between prisoners and their lawyers. As Wiggins opened the door of the room, Brandon got a glimpse of the other inhabitant and froze in his tracks. It was him. A fed, no... *the fed*. The same FBI agent who had put him behind bars and deprived him of the love of his wife, the companionship of his partner in crime and one other thing, there was one other thing that the Fed had done, although unknowingly, but these three reasons were more than enough to earn Jefferson Brown intense hate from Brandon Andrews.

The guards ushered Brandon into the room and closed the door behind him. The two men looked at each other. No words were exchanged for three minutes, after which the Federal agent broke the silence.

"Have a seat Brandon," said Jefferson, waving towards the chair on the other side of the metal table.

Brandon did not budge. "What are you doing here?"

"Sit, Brandon, then we'll talk," Insisted Jefferson.

"There is nothing to talk about," saying this, Brandon turned towards the door when Jefferson's voice made him stop.

"I can get you out of here!"

Brandon turned slowly and said, "What did you just say?"

This time Jefferson did not reply and stared at Brandon. After a second, Brandon gave in and sat down in the chair opposite Jefferson.

"Now we can talk," said Jefferson.

"Look Jefferson, I don't want my time wasted, what were you saying about getting me out of here?"

"Brandon, you are in prison, all you have is time."

"But I can choose how I want to spend it, and I definitely don't choose to spend it in the company of an enemy of mine. Now, what were you talking about?"

"You know as well as I do what I was talking about, I'm offering you a deal."

Brandon was about to say something but then he froze, after an instant a thin smile spread on his lips as he said, "I see, you need my help with the case."

Jefferson looked up sharply and said, "What do you mean?"

"Oh, come on Brown, it is not so difficult. A copycat strikes and whisks away the *Morceaux de Lumiere* from under your nose and then you visit me after years. It is as simple as two plus two, if you're not bad at math."

"You're right, I do need your help, and you're also in desperate need of mine. Without me, you are not getting out of here," said Jefferson.

"I refuse," said Brandon and got up.

"What?" asked Jefferson in disbelief.

"I refuse to help you," said Brandon as though explaining something to a little child.

"I meant both of you."

"*Pardonnez Moi*?" said Brandon in a perfect accent.

"You heard me, I can get both of you out early, *if* you help me catch this thief."

"Thieves," corrected Brandon.

"How do you know that?" asked Jefferson.

"It's not a one-man job."

"That's exactly what I thought."

"Very well Brown, I will help you, but you will need the help of the three of us."

"Three?"

"You're forgetting Claire."

Jefferson did not reply. Suddenly, he didn't want to make eye contact with Brandon.

Brandon said, "What is it?"

"I'm sorry Brandon, but Claire's dead, she died in prison."

Brandon was shocked. The news had put him in a state of distress, but these were times of negotiations, there was no room for emotion.

He controlled his emotions, suppressed his anger and grief, and said, "Fine, then both of us will help you catch them."

"Oh no, your partner gets out of jail early only if *you* help me catch this guy."

Brandon's face turned crimson, and he shouted, "NO BROWN! NO! You deprived me of the love of my wife, she was my partner in everything, she was my better half even on the jobs and guess what? You want my help? Then she gets out with me *while* I help you catch the thief. I won't wait till some rookies are in prison to see the love of my life!"

Jefferson knew that this was going to happen, the man and his wife were an inseparable duo. It was what the romantics called a match made in heaven. Both were gifted thieves, and each loved the other beyond measure.

"Fine, she gets out too, but know this, if you even try anything stupid, I won't hesitate to shoot any of you."

"You never did. Remember last time? You are not human Jefferson, you're a cold machine," said Brandon, venom dripping from his voice.

Jefferson stood up and said, "Had I been that I would not have grazed Claire's thigh, the bullet would have gone through her head."

Brandon lunged at Jefferson with a roar of fury, but Jefferson calmly sidestepped and said, "Touch me and the deal is off, you and the love of your life will rot in prison for the rest of your lives."

Brandon controlled himself at the last moment. "Never threaten me with that again, you need us."

While stepping out of the room, Jefferson said, "Don't forget Brandon, I caught the originals, I can catch the imitators too, you are just a means of speeding up the process."

After Jefferson left, Brandon was escorted back to his cell. Just as Wiggins was about to close the door behind him, Brandon called him.

"Wiggins! I need a favor."

Wiggins turned and said, "What is it?"

"I need newspapers, old ones, at least for the last two weeks."

"You already have them."

"I need different ones, as many as possible."

"Why? Missed a crossword?"

"No, I need to study a specific occurrence."

Wiggins did not ask any more and said that he would see what he could do. After Wiggins was gone, Brandon took a pen and started writing something in his diary. When a person is in solitary confinement the best way to avoid insanity is by writing your thoughts in a diary, at least that was what Brandon believed. He did not hesitate to write anything and everything that he felt and thought in the diary, but that meant that no one was supposed to touch it, *no one*. Brandon was a man whose life was filled with secrets, secrets which were only known to one other person on the face of the planet, his wife. They were going to be together again soon, and out of jail as well. That was something that opened the gate to limitless possibilities. Just as Brandon was writing down this thought in his diary a smile spread on his lips and what he wrote next was something which he had been waiting to write for a long time – *we're back in the game.*

FBI Field Office, NYC:

"What?" exclaimed Sam.

Jefferson was sitting at his desk, while Michael and Sam were sitting in the chairs, opposite to him. He had just told them what he had done earlier that day and Sam had just expressed his surprise with the aid of an exclamation.

Michael sat up a bit straighter and said, "Did I hear this right? You are getting Brandon and Olivia out of prison?"

"Just so they can help us," explained Jefferson.

Sam scoffed and said, "Yeah, as if they wouldn't think of helping themselves! Come on Jefferson, you know what they are capable of, it took years for any law enforcement agency to get them."

"I am very well aware of that, but we need to get the diamonds back."

Michael shook his head and said, "I was thinking about that, the thieves would have already sold off the diamonds, why would they keep them with themselves?"

Jefferson tapped the table and said, "See that is what most people think, but it's not easy, when you have stolen something that has made so much of a buzz, you can't sell it off without taking the risk of alerting the authorities."

"So, they'll just keep the diamonds?"

"At least until the heat has subsided, but that wouldn't stop them from committing another robbery, that is why we need those two."

Sam just shook his head and crossed his arms. Michael made an apologetic expression and said, "Look, Jefferson, I don't mean to be disrespectful but taking the help of *thieves*? That is not very noble." Michael had said the word "thieves" as though it was a condition which was a sign of an inferior human being.

"Michael, nobility is important, but for the sake of nobility, we cannot let thieves and crooks do as they please, the importance of balance is as much as, if not more than, nobility," stated Jefferson in a definitive manner.

Michael and Sam did not say anything else. Taking their silence as acceptance, Jefferson stood up and said, "Now, if you excuse me, I will be on my way to warn a certain businessman that he is about to be robbed of an apparently non-existent collection."

Michael and Sam also stood up, but Jefferson waved a hand and said, "You kids are not coming with me, you have another job to do."

Michael and Sam both looked at each other and groaned. They had hoped to avoid the entire "questioning the inhabitants of the building" thing, but now, it was impossible to do so.

Sam made a futile attempt by saying, "What if someone else did it?"

Jefferson refused by saying, "There is no one else who will be able to do it better than you two."

After Jefferson left, Michael said, "Well, now we need to talk to some uncooperating people who will most likely get annoyed by us."

Sam said, "I have an idea, let's divide the task. I'll do half of the houses on the floor, and you can do the other half, that way we can wind it up faster."

Michael gave Sam a thumbs up and both of them left for the building. Having a job in law enforcement has its pros and cons. There are moments when you will feel as if you are in an action movie, you will feel the rush of adrenaline and your throbbing pulse. There are also times when you will feel like Sherlock Holmes or Hercule Poirot while using your grey cells to solve a case, but then there is the substantial number of the "other times". These "other times" are the times when you have to do boring work like making case notes and interviewing witnesses, with a good chance that a few of them would try their best to annoy you. It was thinking about these "other times" that Michael and Sam made their way to the building.

Once on the floor, the matter was to decide which of the two agents would take the apartments on which side of the corridor. To make this decision, Michael and Sam took the help of a very mature and old way of making decisions – they faced off in an intense match of rock, paper, scissors.

Sam won and chose the apartments on the right, while Michael went and rang the doorbell of the first apartment on the left. He heard a door being opened behind him and after a few words in Sam's voice, he heard the door close again and silence prevailed in the corridor. Michael was left alone, he rang the doorbell again, but getting no answer, he moved to the next apartment. He rang the doorbell and waited. He heard the latch open and a young woman's face looked out of the door. Michael found himself staring at the woman. It was the same woman whom he had seen while waiting for Sam in the car. The same blonde hair and blue eyes, but what Michael was not able to notice the last time were the beautiful and attractive facial features of the woman.

"Yes?" asked the woman in a gentle voice.

"Ma'am my name is Michael Adams, I'm an FBI agent. I would like to ask you a few questions," said Michael, while showing the woman his identification.

The woman stared at Michael for a moment before moving back and opening the door for him. Michael entered the house, and his first impression was that of walking into a small but neat space, with the aroma of lavender in the air.

"Please have a seat, would you like some tea? Coffee?"

"Just water please, thank you," replied Michael while sitting down on the sofa.

The woman disappeared into the kitchen. Michael looked around the room and realized that although the woman was not rich, she had a certain sense which enabled her to arrange what she had in a way that the room looked beautiful.

Suddenly a voice said, "Who are you?"

Michael looked around and saw a boy of about eleven years, who looked startlingly like the woman, standing in the doorway of the room.

"Hello, my name is Michael Adams."

"Who let you in?"

In reply, Michael pointed toward the kitchen. The boy shook his head and said, "I should have known, she is not alert at all, what do you do?"

"I'm an FBI agent."

"Yes, you may be, or you may be an imposter, may I see some ID?" said the kid in an authoritative voice.

Michael could not help but smile. The boy was very thin, and his medium-length hair was ruffled as though he had just walked through a storm. Michael showed him his ID and after inspecting it carefully for a minute, the boy handed it back to him.

"It seems authentic," observed the boy.

"Maybe that's because it is."

"Why are you here?"

"I need to ask her some questions," said Michael pointing toward the kitchen once again.

"She has a name, you know, Evelyn Watson," said the boy and sat down beside Michael on the sofa.

"And is she your mother?"

The boy seemed alarmed by this thought and said, "NO! no, that would have been unbearable, she bosses me around a lot as it is, she's my elder sister."

Michael nodded. Evelyn came out of the kitchen carrying a tray. She placed the tray on the table and said, "Here, I made you some coffee."

She looked at her brother and said, "Why are you sitting here?"

"Remember what I said about bossing me around? Well, this is it," said the boy in Michael's ear.

Michael stifled a laugh. Evelyn was flustered by this statement, and she said, "I apologize for my brother's behavior."

"Oh no, it's quite all right," replied Michael.

"So, what did you want to talk to me about?"

"As you might be aware, the FBI was investigating the apartment at the end of the corridor."

"Oh yes, but I didn't know it was the FBI, it seemed to be quite hush-hush."

"Yes. Well, we would like to know if you happen to know the man who lives there."

"Why is the FBI interested in him?"

"I'm afraid I can't tell you that."

"Well, I didn't even know that some lived in the house."

"Did you happen to see anyone new or unidentified going into or coming out of the apartment?"

"I'm really sorry but, no, I won't be of much help."

Michael let out a sigh. "Very well, ma'am, thank you very much for your time."

Just as he was about to get up, the boy sitting beside him said, "Wait! You didn't ask me."

"Rob..." began Evelyn in a warning tone.

Robert spread his hands and said, "What? A good detective leaves no stone unturned!"

Michael decided to play along with the kid. He liked kids, especially smart kids. "So, Rob, did you know the tenant of that house?"

"No, but I did see someone."

CHAPTER NINE

"Who did you see?" asked Michael.

"I recall details better with some sugar in my system," said Rob, while looking meaningfully at his sister.

Michael understood immediately and said, "Are you really asking for a bribe in the presence of a federal agent?"

"Do you want my help?" asked Rob.

Evelyn groaned and said, "Fine! I'll get you some of those caramel toffees. Now answer the question, please."

Rob smiled happily and said, "From his uniform, he looked like a plumber."

"Did you get a look at his face?" asked Michael.

"Nope, just his back. Sis was at work, and I had gone down to check for any mail in our mailbox."

"How many times have I told you not to go out when you are alone?" asked Evelyn, with a hint of anger in her voice.

"Oh please, I am not a baby, I can take care of myself." Saying this Rob got up from the sofa and in the process, banged his knee on the table. He let out a stifled exclamation but then looked at his sister and ran into the inner room.

Michael stood up and said, "Thank you very much for your time Ma'am."

"Please, call me Evelyn," replied Evelyn as she opened the door for Michael.

As soon as Michael was out of the house, his mind got busy in forming theories. He asked the other tenants a few questions but most of them were as clueless as Evelyn. Finally, he exited the last apartment to find Sam waiting for him at the other end of the hall.

Just as Michael walked up to him, Sam said, "Well, I have absolutely zero leads so far, what about you? Somewhere close by?"

"Actually, I do have something," said Michael. "A kid saw someone entering the apartment."

"Who? Did he look at his face?"

"Nope, just his back. The kid says he looked like a plumber, judging by his uniform."

"Well, that is something, at least we know how he entered the apartment to set the stage."

Michael and Sam had exited the building by now and were getting seated in the car.

"So even you think it was one of the thieves?" asked Michael.

"Who else could it be? Why would anyone call the plumber in a house where no one lives?"

Michael nodded. After a moment he said, "Well, from tomorrow we are going to have some extra help as well."

"We don't need any help. We'll catch the thieves ourselves."

"Even if we don't need it, we are going to have to put up with those thieves. I believe we better keep an eye on them," said Michael.

"You got it," replied Sam, then after a moment, he added, "I wonder how Jefferson is getting along."

Williamson Residence, NYC:
Jefferson had just reached the house of Harold Williamson and presented his credentials when he was let

in by Mr. Williamson's personal butler. Jefferson was made to sit in the living room, and after an impatient wait of five minutes, Harold Williamson entered the room. After a brief handshake, the two gentlemen took a seat facing each other. Harold Williamson was a middle-aged man with gray hair. His physique was closer in appearance to a basketball player than a businessman due to his tall features. He was dressed in a black suit as though he was attending a board meeting rather than meeting an FBI agent.

"Well, Agent Jefferson, here I am. What can I do for you?" asked Harold.

"On the contrary, Mr. Williamson, it is something that we would like to do for you."

"What do you mean?"

"I mean that we have reason to believe that a robbery will be committed with the intention of stealing some items of your personal collection and we would like to prevent that."

The businessman looked at Jefferson for a few moments with a blank expression. Then he said, "I'm afraid there is a misunderstanding, I'm not the owner of any personal collection."

"Are you quite sure of that Mr. Williamson? Because if you try to hide something and, in the process, refuse our assistance, you may be sorry later."

Mr. Williamson looked up sharply and said, "Is that a threat?"

"Certainly not, it is a warning. The thieves who have claimed to steal several items of your personal collection are among the most skilled I have ever encountered in my career."

The businessman was about to say something when an elegantly dressed woman entered the room. She walked up to Mr. Williamson and said, "I hope everything is all right my dear?"

"Of course, it is just some misunderstanding, the agent here seems to think that I have a private collection of some sort and it is going to be stolen."

Perhaps it was Jefferson's imagination, but for a moment he thought as though the woman's face had gone pale. She said, "Stolen?"

"Don't you worry, my dear, if it doesn't exist, it cannot be stolen!" said Mr. Williamson and laughed loudly.

Jefferson said, "Do you have any idea what the thieves could be referring to as your personal collection?"

Mr. Williamson thought for a moment before answering. He said, "Nothing comes to my mind, do you have any idea what it could mean, Alice?"

His wife did not answer and kept staring at the floor. It was only when her husband called her name for the second time that she said, "Oh what? No, I don't have any idea."

Jefferson looked at her and felt as though she was hiding something. Something important, yet he could not accuse her without any evidence. He got up and said, "Very well Mr. Williamson, if you happen to think of anything then just give me a call, here is my card."

Mr. Williamson took the card and laid it on the side table without giving it a second look. Jefferson exited the residence of the businessman and soon found himself sitting in his car and staring at the road. Try as he might, he could not shake off the feeling that Alice Williamson knew something, but if she did not divulge the information during the talk, then it was quite obvious that she was averse to the idea of sharing the information with Jefferson. Jefferson started the car and eased it out of the parking space. There weren't many ways to ask someone if they were hiding something. Then there was another option altogether, which eliminated the need to ask the person in question anything at all.

As soon as Jefferson reached his office, he summoned Michael and Sam. It appeared that both of them were just waiting for him to arrive as they burst out talking as soon as they saw him.

Jefferson raised a hand to silence them and said, "Relax, both of you. What is it that you have found?"

"We think we know how the thief managed to arrange the apartment as we saw it," said Michael.

"He did it as a plumber!" said Sam unable to wait any longer to break the news.

"A what?"

"We think he disguised himself as a plumber and went into the house. Then he made all the necessary arrangements and departed the building," explained Michael.

"And how do you know this?"

"A kid told Michael."

"A kid? How old?"

Michael grew nervous. He said, "Around Eleven."

"Eleven? You are forming theories based on what an eleven-year-old kid told you?"

"He is a pretty smart kid," said Michael.

Sam said, "Come on Jefferson, you never judged a person based on their age before, why do it now?"

Michael nodded. "Plus, what he said is the only useful thing we learned."

Jefferson looked at the two men sitting in front of him and realized something for the first time. Sam was trusting Michael. He had not talked to the boy, but he was willing to accept what the boy had said, just because Michael thought that it was reliable information. Initially, he had been reluctant to agree with Michael, but now, after seeing that the two agents had begun to work together in a true sense for the very first time, he decided not to say anything else.

Jefferson nodded and said, "All right, let's take that as a working hypothesis for now. There is something I want you to do."

"What is it?" asked Sam.

"I need you to look into Alice Williamson."

"Harold Williamson's wife?" asked Michael.

"Yes, I think she is hiding some information."

"And Harold is not aware of anything?"

"Well, to me, he looked genuinely surprised, but you can never be too sure. His wife, however, went pale when I mentioned the private collection."

Sam agreed and said, "I'll look into it, and there is one more thing. The reports came back from the analysis of the blood they found on the wall of the apartment. Turns out, it wasn't blood, it was paint, made specifically to match the color of blood as closely as possible."

Jefferson just nodded but Michael turned towards Sam and said, "Specifically made?"

"Yeah, it is a tint which is not quite common. Many companies don't even offer that color."

"That means the thieves must have acquired it specifically for this set up?"

"Yes, so what?" asked Sam impatiently, "Maybe the guy has a flair for theatricality."

"My point is that they would have ordered the paint from somewhere and most probably quite recently, so this is an opportunity for *us* to track *them*."

Jefferson looked at Michael and said, "That's quite an idea. Get as much information as you can about the paint and where can it be bought from."

Michael and Sam got up. Jefferson said, "Michael, you stay for a moment, there is something I want to talk to you about."

This was an odd instruction. Michael looked at Sam who exchanged a meaningful look with Jefferson and left.

Jefferson said, "Michael I won't beat around the bush. I just wanted to know how you're holding up."

Michael knew exactly what he was talking about, but still, he said, "What are you talking about?"

"Michael, alcohol withdrawal can be quite brutal, are you feeling all right?"

"Oh yes, I'm just drinking a lot of fluids, it's not easy, but I won't lose to my temptations."

Jefferson replied, "That's quite brave, what you are doing, and I respect you for that."

Michael left Jefferson's office. As soon as Michael went out, Jefferson received a text on his cellphone. It was from an unidentified number. The message was only two words long – *Hello Jefferson.*

CHAPTER TEN

A Hotel in NYC:

Oliver and Calvin were sitting in a hotel room and Oliver was typing furiously at his computer keyboard. After waiting for about twenty minutes, Calvin decided to ask Oliver exactly what it was that he was doing.

"You better not be playing a video game," said Calvin in his deep voice.

Oliver looked up from the computer screen and said, "Why must you disturb me exactly when I am doing something important? Didn't you have to arrange some uniforms for us?"

"Relax, I am the best at what I do, the uniforms are taken care of."

Oliver nodded approvingly and said, "In that case, I can tell you what I'm doing. I am currently chatting with the agent who hopes to put us behind bars."

Calvin looked up sharply and said, "What? You are talking to Jefferson Brown?"

"Chatting, not talking. But yes, the name is correct."

Calvin got up and walked over to where Oliver was seated. He stood behind him so that he could get a clear view of his screen.

After trying to understand what was going on for a few minutes and failing miserably, Calvin said, "How are you chatting with him?"

"I have a program that uses the internet to send text messages. That way he wouldn't know who is on the other end."

"But can't he trace the message back to us?"

"No, he can't, I am bouncing the signal all over the globe."

Calvin looked satisfied. His partner was like him, the best at what he did.

"What message did you send?"

Instead of replying, Oliver pointed towards the top right area of his screen where a message was showing – *Hello Jefferson*

A moment later another message popped up below that, this time it was from Jefferson – **Who is this?**

I think you know.

Why contact me like this? Too afraid to show yourself?

These primitive psychological tricks won't work on me.

After this message, Oliver did not receive any reply. He waited five seconds and then said, "Right now he is running around and trying to get hold of someone who can try to track me."

After two minutes, Oliver received a new message – **You still there, copycat?**

I am still here, former protector of Les Morceaux de Lumiere :D

I will get you, you little fool.

Quit stalling. You can't track me, now listen, I'm warning you, if you come after me, the only thing you will get is embarrassment.

We know how you pulled off the heist, we are on your trail.

The trail that ended with Ra<u>fool</u> E<u>d</u>munds?

You have twenty-four hours to surrender.

And you have a few days to prevent a robbery, that is, if you ever find out about the collection.

This will end with you in handcuffs.

The fun has barely begun agent.

Bring it on.

You better buckle up, it's going to be quite a ride.

After this message, Oliver terminated the connection. There was nothing more to be said, both sides had tried to intimidate each other but were not sure if they had succeeded or not. However, Oliver was confident that the plan was perfect.

Calvin said, "What did he mean that they were onto us?"

"Relax, they were bluffing. Ask your contact who has been keeping an eye on Harold if Jefferson visited him today."

Calvin sent a message and received a reply almost instantly. He read the message and said, "Yes, he did."

"Then that is what Jefferson meant, they don't have anything else."

"You better be right."

"I usually am."

FBI Field Office, NYC:

The man sitting at the computer waited for a few moments. He had to be sure before he said anything. Finally, he said, "The connection is terminated. The trace failed."

Jefferson slapped the table with his open palm. Michael let out a breath he had been holding. The only inhabitants of the room were Michael, Sam, Jefferson, and the man who had been trying to trace the source of the connection. To state the obvious, the situation in the room was tense. While everyone was quiet, the guy from tech support quickly got up and left, excusing himself from a very awkward situation. Michel and Sam were at a loss for words. They did not know what to say to make Jefferson feel better without making him feel offended.

"There was one good thing about that," said Michael.

"What was that?" asked Jefferson. "I think I missed it."

"They don't know about the paint. They think our trail ended with Rafool Edmunds."

Sam said, "That's not much of a lead."

"And yet that is exactly why they overlooked it, it is their first mistake and our best chance at getting them."

"Our best chance will be with us by tomorrow morning," stated Jefferson as he left the room.

Sam looked at Michael and said, "So I guess we are still getting the help from the convicts."

Michael did not reply. Sam stared at him and said, "Hello? Michael?"

"Yeah?"

"I said we are still getting the help from the convicts."

"Yeah, right," said Michael before leaving the room.

The truth was that he had not heard a word that Sam had said. His mind was elsewhere, he could not help but think that the package he had received the previous night had something to do with the thieves. He had not told anyone about it yet, in fact, he had convinced himself that it was some foolish prank by some kid. But now he was forced to reconsider his opinions. Yet, there were two things that did not make sense, why go through the trouble of delivering a physical package when the thieves could have contacted him through digital means and thus, reduced the chances of getting caught and the second and more pressing question was, why contact him? What could he do?

Maximum Security Women's Prison:

Olivia Andrews was pacing her cell. She was a beautiful woman to the extent that even the years in prison had done little to suppress her attractive features. Her black hair was cut such that the length was till the mid-point of her neck, and her hazel eyes were constantly shifting focus from one thing to another. On her bed lay an unfinished Sudoku puzzle and that was an indication of the seriousness of the matter. Once she started solving a puzzle, she never left it unfinished, but today was different. Her boring and monotonous routine had been interrupted by a call. She had received a call from her husband, which was an exceedingly rare pleasure and that call had changed her perspective towards life. Usually, she spent her time thinking about the past, but now, it appeared, she had a future to think of. Her mind was constantly replaying the conversation she had with her husband, a conversation regarding a deal that was offered to them by the same man who was responsible for their separation and incarceration. But still, a deal was a deal, you did something, and you got something in return, there was no need to like the other party.

Some people get reformed in prison, some people become bitter, and their case worsens, but some people, the rare ones, remain unchanged. They are the ones who silently bid their time and dream about the wonderful, wonderful for them, things they would do when they got out. Olivia stopped pacing and took up the sudoku puzzle once again. She looked at the numbers, but her brain was thinking about the moment when she would finally see her husband again and get to step out of the prison. That was an idea which opened an infinite number of possibilities for her. A smile spread on her lips as she realized that this was the same thought that must have crossed her husband's mind.

CHAPTER ELEVEN

The next day Michael reached the bureau early. He had just kept his bag on his desk when Sam looked into his cubicle. Both exchanged a nod and continued with their respective tasks. Each of them knew why the other was early, it was obvious. Although they were against the idea of getting felons out of prison and taking their help, they could not miss the opportunity to see Jefferson walk in with the two infamous thieves for the first time. Even though both knew Brandon and Olivia were criminals, they could not overlook the fact that they were legendary criminals. The number of perfect robberies they had committed was commendable and to think that no one even knew their identities before they were caught was something even more amazing.

Try as they might, Michael and Sam could not get their head into their work. Michael kept checking his watch and Sam was continuously staring at the door. Finally, they saw Jefferson open the glass door and usher a man and a woman in. Michael noticed that both the convicts were fitted with devices to monitor their location at all times. To be more precise, they were given ankle monitors. Brandon walked in and immediately sat down on one of the chairs as though he owned the place. Olivia kept standing and looking at the people around her with interest. When she looked at Michael, she stared at him for a moment longer than the others with an odd expression on her face, but perhaps that was because Michael had an expression on his face that clearly expressed that he found the company of two criminals repulsive.

Jefferson said, "Michael, Sam, meet Brandon and Olivia Andrews, they will be assisting us with the case."

"Hello Michelle, hello Samantha, how do you do?" asked Brandon and laughed.

Olivia said, "Now, don't be rude dear. They're just children."

Michael stepped forward and said, "We are federal agents and that means we have the authority to throw you back in jail as and when we please."

Olivia laughed and said, "You may have the authority, but do you have the permission? You need us."

Michael looked at Jefferson and the latter shrugged his shoulders.

Sam said, "Jefferson, are they here to waste our time?"

"Absolutely not," replied Jefferson. "They're here to work, now let me show you where the two of you will be working."

Jefferson pointed towards a large table that had recently been set up near the coffee machine. Brandon looked at it and raised an eyebrow.

"You really expect us to work there?" he asked.

"Yes, and I don't ask, I *tell you* what you need to do," said Jefferson in an authoritative manner.

While the couple made their way towards the table, a single thought was going through the mind of each of the three agents, they had to be alert at all times.

Precisely fifteen minutes later, the agents and the former thieves were talking about various aspects of the case. Jefferson had told the two consultants what they had learned so far and what were their theories. For the first time, Brandon and Olivia seemed to be genuinely interested, they were listening intently and responding with enthusiasm.

Brandon said, "These guys are smart and sophisticated. From the way they stole the diamonds, it is evident that they prefer to use brains and this type of thieves are the hardest to catch."

"Agreed," said Olivia "From what you have told us so far, they have managed to outsmart you twice and now, the best lead you have is the custom-made paint."

Michael nodded. "Yes, the paint is a rare shade of blood red. From what I have found out, there are only eleven places in America from where you could get that shade without having the chance of getting caught later."

"Out of those places, how many are in NYC?" asked Brandon.

"Just Three, why?"

"Because it would have been easier to buy it in NYC, rather than get it from another state," explained Olivia.

Jefferson looked at Olivia and said, "So are you saying that they got the paint from one of those three places?"

"Exactly."

"I'll look into it," said Michael.

"I'll help," said Brandon, getting up.

"I never said I needed the help of a crook to catch another."

"All right, that's enough," said Jefferson. "If we want to catch these guys, we need to cooperate. Brandon, you go with Michael. Olivia, you and Sam will look into Alice Williamson."

Sam groaned and said, "What about you?"

"Sometimes I forget, who is the senior one here?" asked Jefferson with a hint of a smile and walked away.

The ones who were left behind looked at their partners. Multiple opinions were exchanged but no words were uttered. It was all done with the assistance of facial muscles. After a few minutes, Michael left, and to his dismay, Brandon followed him. The man was aware that his presence irritated Michael, but he seemed to enjoy testing the limits of Michael's patience.

Once Brandon and Michael were on their way, the former kept staring at the latter. Michael tried to ignore the stare, but he found himself getting distracted by it and in the end, he concluded that a direct confrontation was the best and the shortest approach.

"Stop staring."

"Staring helps me think," replied Brandon in a sing-song voice.

"Then stare outside the window."

"What is your problem with me?"

"Well, apart from the fact that you are a convicted felon who insists on behaving like a child all day long, there isn't much against you."

"Being a felon does not necessarily mean that I'm a bad person."

"Oh, of course, they just locked you up for your unusual choice of a career."

"You know what I mean. I was a thief, not a man who hurts others like serial killers, who I guarantee, are awfully bad men."

"There is something you need to understand, as long as you talk to me about something that is relevant to the case, you may expect a reply, however, if you attempt to talk to me about anything else, be prepared to withstand absolute silence."

"All right, partner, let's talk about the case. We need to pull a con."

"Excuse me?"

"You heard me, I hate to disappoint you, but your dreams of barging in and flashing your badge and getting answers straightaway are never going to be fulfilled."

"And exactly what do you propose we do?"

"You can be my son."

"What?"

"You will be my son, one of those fanatics who think that the color of blood is cool, you will be arguing with me about the color of the paint, quite loudly, and saying that you were willing to pay anything for the paint of that specific shade and your friend recently bought it from that very place."

"So, the shopkeeper would either agree or disagree and that would tell us if he did sell the paint to anyone."

"Glad to see that you are trying to keep up."

"Glad to see that you have brains."

After the minute hand of the watch had made a few more rounds, the two men reached the first shop. It was one of those home décors shops that offered everything, from Sofa sets to curtains.

Michael entered the shop with a moody expression on his face but then he stopped. Brandon came in behind him and stopped too. Both of them looked at each other, Brandon raised an eyebrow, but Michael exited

"So, tell me," said Brandon as they got back into the car.

"Tell you what?"

"You know what, why didn't you proceed to question the owner?"

"Because the thieves didn't get the paint from there."

Brandon said, "Please tell me it was a little more than a gut feeling."

Michael sighed and said, "Fine, that wasn't the type of place where a thief would go to buy something. There were CCTV cameras and a proper system for making transactions. The state of all these items made it obvious that they were properly maintained. Now, firstly, no one would go through so much trouble if their business wasn't good and someone with a good business and who believed in making secure transactions wouldn't risk taking part in any sort of illegal activity so the chances of him cooperating with thief were low, and it would not have been possible for the thieves to come and go undetected or without leaving a trace because of the stringent security measures."

After this monologue, Brandon nodded his head as though he was impressed. "Not bad, Michael, not bad at all."

"Thanks, your opinion *really* matters to me."

With the first place stricken off the list, the unconventional duo headed towards the second place on their list. This second place was an old paint shop. Very old. The man who owned it was almost as ancient, and one look at it would have convinced anyone that it was an ideal spot for getting something without leaving a trail.

Michael entered the shop and said, "I told you, Dad, I want to choose the color myself."

Brandon shook his head and said, "And I said you can, but choose anything except red."

"It's not just red, custom-made blood red, that's what I want."

The owner of the shop came up to the two men and said, "Let it go, sir, the kids these days, they all want the same things."

Brandon sighed and said, "I don't think anyone would be naive enough to buy blood-coloured paint, it's stupid, not to mention it's difficult to acquire."

"I will pay whatever amount is necessary to get what I want, but I won't settle for anything else," said Michael in a definitive tone.

The old man's eyes lit up. The paint business was not exactly the most rewarding and when a stubborn kid walked in, it was a sign that the man could sell the paints for a little more than usual.

The old man said, "You see, sir, the paint is quite expensive, it is of the top quality but not many people buy it, so it's made on order."

Brandon looked at Michael and said, "See? Not many people buy it, it will be ages before you get it. Want to change your mind?"

The old man interjected and said, "Oh no sir, luckily I just sold some to a client, I even have a can with me, you can buy it right away, but as I said, it will be expensive."

Michael shrugged and said, "Money is not a problem, but I don't want old paint, something that you have in the back of your storage for years."

"Oh no sir, I sold it to a gentleman just a few weeks ago!"

Michael looked at Brandon at this statement. They had what they wanted, now it was time to drop the façade.

Michael said, "Tell me, sir, have you heard of the FBI?"

"Who hasn't?"

"Well, that makes it easier. My name is Michael Adams, I'm an FBI special agent and the man you sold the paint to is a suspect in a robbery."

The old man's demeanor changed drastically. Within a moment he had transformed from a cunning salesman to a god-fearing citizen of the country.

He said, "I'm afraid I don't remember much sir, it's this old age."

"Do you know the FBI interrogation rooms specialize in memory problems?"

Brandon nodded and said, "I can tell you from experience, they really are quite good."

"I said I don't remember *much*, but I do remember the man, his appearance and his name."

"That is all we want," said Michael, and indicated towards a chair in the man's office.

The man sat down and said, "The name of the man was John D."

"Full name?" asked Michael.

"I didn't ask, he paid me pretty well to avoid sharing the details," said the man awkwardly.

Brandon said, "No need to guess, I know what his full name was – John Doe, they have quite a good sense of humor."

"Do you remember the man's features?"

"Yes, I don't forget a good customer."

Michael said, "Get up. You need to come with us and talk to a sketch artist."

Brandon stopped Michael and said, "Relax, I'm not just a thief. There was a time when I was an art student, and I'm quite good. We don't have to waste any more time."

Five minutes later, Brandon was seated opposite the old man who was trying to describe the face of the man with the help of words. Michael was standing over Brandon's shoulder and although he didn't say anything, he was quite impressed by the man's skill. He was doing a remarkable job of converting what he was being told into a picture. His hand was steady and precise as a surgeon's, and his concentration was unwavering. Within forty-five minutes most of the sketch was done and Michael could see the face of one of the thieves. That was not the part that excited Michael. It was something else that did. He had seen the man before.

CHAPTER TWELVE

Residence of the Williamson Family, NYC:

Mrs. Williamson was seated on the bed, in her room. Her palms felt clammy and the air around her felt cold. She was suffering from anxiety, and she knew it, and she also knew why. She had called her son thrice, but her son had not answered. He was currently in London, sent there by his father for business purposes and he was due to come back the next day, but she could not wait. What she had to tell him was important. There was a knock on the door and her husband entered, walked over to where his wife was sitting and sat down beside her.

"Alice, are you feeling all right?"

"Oh yes, just tired, I suppose."

"Well, you certainly look the part. Why don't you lie down? If you want, I can call the doctor."

Alice placed a hand on her husband's arm and said, "No need for that, I'm quite all right, although I think lying down would be a good idea."

Harold stood up and said, "I'll leave you to it then. Take care."

Harold kissed his wife's forehead and then exited the room. Alice's head had just hit the pillow when her phone rang. The call was from her son. She received the call at once.

"Where have you been Jack? I have called you thrice."

"Relax Mom, I was in a meeting. What's the matter?"

"You need to come back."

"I'm coming back tomorrow evening."

"You need to come back *today*."

"Mom, you're scaring me, is everything all right?" asked Jack in a concerned voice.

"No, nothing is all right, it's about the *Animalia*."

Now the tone of Jack's voice changed. "What about it?"

"Just come back." Alice implored her son.

"I'll be on the next flight out of here," said Jack, and hung up.

Alice placed the phone on her bedside table and tried to sleep. After ten minutes she sat up in bed with a frustrated sigh. Her mind was far too disturbed to be able to rest. She reached for the drawer in her bedside table and extracted a medicine from it. She took a tablet with a sip of water and then lay down again. This time her worries were neutralized by the soothing effects of the medicine, and she was soon in a deep slumber.

A luxury Hotel, London:

Jack Williamson was sitting in a chair and thinking. He had just called his secretary to his room, as he needed to clear his schedule for the day. He had more important things to address, things that could not wait.

The secretary knocked on the door and then entered. She was a woman in her late twenties. She was dressed smartly, as always, in a business suit.

"How may I assist you, sir?"

"Janice, I want you to clear my schedule for the day and book a ticket to New York, I'm going back home."

"But sir, you have two meetings today, your father..."

"I can deal with my father. You need to deal with the people who were scheduled to meet me today."

"What reason should I give for your unavailability sir?"

"Tell them anything, just make sure that they don't bother me."

"Right away sir, what time would you like to leave?"

"As soon as possible."

The secretary exited and Jack fell into thought once again. His father would not be happy with his decision. He wanted everything to be perfect and cancelling the meetings was far from it. But then there was the other thing, the *Animalia*, if his father found out about that, then things would get very bad, very quick. He dialed a number on his phone, it was a number he had not saved, rather, one that he had memorized. He even deleted the call from the logs later. Jack was a careful man, if he didn't want to leave a trail, he didn't. The man he was calling received the call on the third ring.

"Where are you?" asked Jack.

"At the property, Sir."

"Is there any problem?"

"None at all Sir, everything is perfectly fine."

"Very well, I'll be dropping by soon to check on everything."

"Sure sir, anytime."

Jack terminated the call and got ready. His mother was right, this thing was worth going back immediately.

FBI Field Office, NYC:

Sam had been patient for a long time but now he was starting to lose it. The reason for his irritation was sitting right in front of him, namely, Olivia Andrews. She was one of the people who could do other things while concentrating on their work the whole time, unfortunately, she decided to use this ability to make fun of her immediate partner. Whenever Sam said something or did something, she would not misbehave, rather she would reply very sweetly, a little too sweetly, as she talked to Sam as though she was talking to a dim-witted child. Her manner clearly indicated that she saw Sam as an intellectually inferior being, although this was not true. In the little time she had spent with Sam, she had realized that he had potential, but the problem was that he was a federal agent. Had he been anything other than a fed, Olivia felt sure that they could have been friends, but his occupation was such that Olivia could not help but dislike him, and this dislike resulted in her tendencies to make fun of him.

That was what was going on in the interpersonal relationship area. But on the work front, their progress was quite remarkable. They had dug into old files and internet records of the entire Williamson family and had amassed the history of every existing member, namely, Harold, Alice, and Jack. Harold came out clean, he had a few run-ins with the law here and there but they were all business-related occurrences. To sum it up in a few words, he was as clean as a businessman could be. His wife was as clean as her husband. Before marriage she had been the only daughter of a rich family, the marriage did bring in some financial benefits for Harold, but it was evident from their various social media posts that the husband and wife were still head over heels in love with each other. She was very well educated, but after marriage, she had chosen to become a housewife rather than choose entrepreneurship which was the obvious choice for anyone with her qualifications.

The most interesting member of the family, from the investigative point of view, was Jack Williamson. Like both of his parents, he had been well educated and had taken in his father's footsteps to expand the business. Initially, there had been some media reports about the strained relationship between the father and son but over time, it appeared, their relationship had improved. The son had become more sincere towards work and the father had decided to cut him some slack. That was where the normal part ended. If one looked upon the man's financials from the eye of an officer or a detective, one would not have found anything, but when his financials were scrutinized under the eye of a skilled thief and a con woman like Olivia, his secrets were no longer secrets.

After looking over Jack's financials for some time, Olivia said, "There's something wrong here."

Sam looked up from the file he was reading and said, "What?"

"The money he earns always goes into his bank account and usually this is the salary he gets from his father's company, but look at this, there are some instances when his salary does not get credited into his bank account and it doesn't even get compensated anywhere."

Sam realized that Olivia was not talking to him as though he was a child. She was serious and that meant what she had found was of importance.

"So, what does it mean?" asked Sam.

"It's highly unusual that he would not realize that his salary was not credited to his bank and that means he knows exactly where that money is going, and he had no problem with it."

"You mean that it is possible that he is the one who is utilizing the money somewhere else."

"Very good Sam, you are making progress!" said Olivia in an exaggerated manner.

Sam sighed. Now he was sure that she was one of the people who could not control themselves. When they wanted to do something, they just had to do it.

Sam said, "Can you not control yourself for two minutes?"

"What happened dear?" asked Olivia.

"That..." said Sam pointing towards Olivia's mouth "...that happened. Can't you talk normally and be serious for just five minutes?"

"I am serious, my dear, I always am."

Sam was about to say something when Jefferson walked over to where they were working.

"I have some good news. Michael says that he may have the sketch of one of the thieves," said Jefferson

"Brilliant!" exclaimed Sam. "How did he get it?"

"I don't know the details myself, but he says that they are just reaching so we'll get the entire story soon," said Jefferson.

Olivia said, "Good. Even we have something."

Jefferson looked at Sam and the latter shrugged as if to say, 'Maybe or maybe not'.

"Okay, what have you got?"

"In a formal way, the results of our investigation indicate that the husband and wife are clear however the financial record of their son contains some discrepancies. In an informal way, we need to question the kid."

"We can't just barge in and question someone. We need to have proof. What sort of discrepancies?" asked Jefferson.

Olivia shook her head. "Police procedure, you need proof to question a suspect, you need warrants to search houses. No wonder you took so much time to get us."

"Well, we prefer not to be called intruders or robbers or illegal detainers as those are the descriptions of the people whom we put behind bars," retorted Jefferson.

Sam laughed and said, "Good one Jefferson!"

Olivia looked at Sam and said, "Would you like to do the explaining dear or should I do it? Seeing that I was the one who found the discrepancies."

Sam frowned at her but did not say anything.

She said, "That's what I thought."

Olivia then proceeded to explain to Jefferson what she had found and what she and Sam suspected. After the explaining was done, Jefferson was quiet for a long time. Then he stood up and started pacing.

Finally, after fifteen minutes he said, "Nope. There is no way we can detain him just based on some discrepancies in his account. We need something directly connected to the case."

Sam said, "But that would take time to find, that is assuming we do find anything."

Olivia was silent. This was something that she did when she was thinking. Only then did she think that it was necessary for her to rest her lips and exercise her brain. After meticulously thinking over the problem, she made a connection.

"Well, we don't know what he is guilty of, but he knows," said Olivia. "And from what Jefferson told me, so does his mother."

"How do you know again?" asked Sam.

"Because when I mentioned the collection, his mother paled but his father did not even flinch," replied Jefferson.

"Precisely. So, we can assume that the collection has something to do with her son or more probably, her son owns the collection."

"That's good thinking," complemented Jefferson. "But we know for sure that his father doesn't know about the collection, and since the father is the strict one, we can assume that it is on the outskirts of the law if not entirely illegal."

"If you are right and the collection is illegal, then even if it is stolen, he won't be able to report it, that's why the thieves told us about it. The thieves could have just stolen it without anyone knowing but they told us about the collection so that we uncover it and then when the thieves try to steal it, will be headlines."

"All that is fine, but the question still remains, how do we get him to tell us where he keeps the stuff?"

Olivia, being the ex-thief, had a solution for the problem which was also 'on the outskirts of the law'.

"We call up his mother and tell her that her son's collection will be stolen," she said.

"Call her up? We don't have any proof that her son owns the collection or for that matter, any collection," said Sam.

"We don't call her up as feds..." began Olivia.

"You are *not* a fed," muttered Sam.

Olivia chose to ignore this remark and proceeded, "... we call her up as the thieves."

Jefferson looked at her sharply and said, "We are federal agents, we don't resort to stuff like that."

Olivia smiled and said, "Like Sam just said, not every one of us is a federal agent, in fact, some of us are cons...ex-cons."

Jefferson looked at her and after a moment, said, "I didn't know anything about this."

"Nor did I," said Sam.

Olivia rubbed her hands together and said, "I take that as a yes."

Just as Olivia finished this sentence Michael and Brandon came in. They walked up to where the other three were seated.

Jefferson said, "Where's the sketch?"

Michael was thinking hard. He absentmindedly handed Jefferson the paper, Sam noticed this and said, "You don't look like you're the one who has made a breakthrough."

Michael did not reply, Brandon did. "That's because he thinks he knows the man in the picture, but he cannot remember who he is."

CHAPTER THIRTEEN

Jefferson looked at Michael with astonishment. He said, "What do you mean you cannot remember?"

"I mean I have seen his face before. I just cannot remember who he is," said Michael in a strained voice.

"Have you met him before?" asked Sam.

"No, I don't think so, I just know his face, probably from a photograph," said Michael.

"That means one of two things," said Jefferson.

"Which are?" prompted Brandon.

"Either the man is very famous and had his photograph in the papers, which is highly unlikely, as, if that was the case one of us would have also recognized him. The second case is that Michael has seen his photograph in some old case file of his. Any other source would not have triggered his memory under such circumstances, if he had seen the man in a personal photograph, he would have known the man personally and it's impossible to forget someone like that. On the other hand, if he had just met him somewhere, it is highly unlikely that he would have remembered his face till date."

"Then old case file it is," declared Brandon

"Old case file? He must have worked a ton of cases!" exclaimed Olivia.

All of a sudden, Michael seemed to be nervous. He said, "Actually I've not been very busy for some time, and if I vaguely remember the man's face, that means the case must have been one of the last cases I worked on, I'll check the files."

Jefferson nodded and said, "Good, now Olivia has a plan that all of us are unaware of."

Michael immediately understood what was going on. "I don't even want to know what it is about."

Olivia said, "Before Jefferson refused to hear my plan, I was about to tell him that I wanted to call Alice Williamson pretending to be the thief and tell her that her son's collection would be stolen."

"Son's collection? Why?" asked Michael.

Jefferson looked meaningfully at Sam. "Sam, why don't you go and help Michael with his old files? And don't tell him what Olivia's plan was."

Sam grinned as he left with Michael. After they were gone, Olivia said, "I suppose I won't tell you the time when I would have called the wife?"

"Of course not, I already forbade you to do it," said Jefferson.

Brandon said, "Enough of this game, tell me you're going to hold up your end of the deal."

"I am."

"We need a guarantee," said Olivia.

"I *am* the guarantee. If you help me get the thieves, I will get your sentence reduced."

"Sentence reduced? I want to get out of there!" exclaimed Brandon.

"And you will, but after some time, and be thankful that you are getting out *at all*," said Jefferson and walked away.

Now Brandon and Olivia were left alone. Brandon said, "They call *us* thieves and we are the ones being cheated."

"And they call themselves officers of the law," scoffed Olivia. "They don't know anything about justice."

Brandon looked at his wife and said, "I missed you, a lot."

"So did I and don't worry, we'll be together soon, and free," said Olivia in a hopeful voice. "And maybe even..."

"Don't say it. Please don't, it's painful. It's best if we stay away ...for all of us," said Brandon.

Olivia just nodded.

Brandon said, "Let's just hope we catch these guys."

"We will, we have no choice," said Olivia darkly.

Some distance away, Sam had just finished Explaining to Michael what Olivia planned to do and why she had planned to do it. Once he was finished, Sam took a deep breath. It had been quite a long explanation.

Michael said, "So I guess those two are being helpful after all."

"Yeah, I guess so, anyway, let's thumb through these files."

Michael nodded and they set to work. Before his problem with alcohol had started, Michael had worked on quite a few cases, and going through all of them was some task. The easier way would have been to search the digital records but since all they had was a sketch based on the description of an old man who was not very fond of observing details, the digital search would not have been fruitful.

While working, Sam said, "This almost reminds me of the painting from London."

"What?" asked Michael.

"Don't you know? Oh, I think you were on holiday or something, your parents were shifting. It was over a year ago, someone stole a few valuable paintings from the

London Art Gallery. It was an almost impossible job, like this one."

"Now that you mention it, I did see the coverage on the news. You think it was the same thieves?"

Sam thought for a moment, then said, "No, I don't think so."

"Why not?"

"Because they challenged Jefferson, it doesn't make sense to commit a robbery in London if you want to challenge a federal agent in the USA."

Some more minutes passed in silence, until Sam found what they were looking for.

"Here we go, this is the guy, isn't it?"

Michael took the file from Sam's hand and studied the photograph. Then he nodded with satisfaction. "Now, I remember, Calvin Dowers, small-time actor turned drug dealer and murderer, he'd been given a death sentence, but he escaped during a prison transfer."

"But that was all when he was very young, quite some time ago, how did you get to work on this case?"

"There was some new lead, he was involved in a gang murder or something, but he got away again and since then, he had completely dropped out of the picture."

"Until now," said Sam.

"Until now," agreed Michael. "Come on, let's get this to Jefferson."

The two agents walked up to Jefferson's office and knocked on the door. Receiving the permission to enter, they opened the door and Michael placed the file on Jefferson's desk.

Jefferson picked up the file and read it. "Calvin Dowers, now I remember him. He was the one who escaped during prison custody. You sure it's our guy?"

"Positive," said Michael.

"There is just one thing that bothers me, why would he be interested in a jewel robbery? The only things he was interested in were drug dealing and extortion."

Sam said, "We can ask him that when we catch him, let's get his address and get him."

"No," said Jefferson.

"What?" asked Michael with disbelief. "He's one of the thieves."

"Exactly, he is *one* of the thieves, even if we go and get him, we might end up alerting his partners and lose him and we don't know which one of them may have the diamonds."

"Then what do we do?" asked Michael.

"We keep this quiet. This is an advantage, we now know the identity of one of the thieves and we know his name. We try to locate him and then tail him so that he leads us to his partner or partners."

"All right, we'll get on it," said Michael and he and Sam were about to leave when Michael stopped and said, "Where are Brandon and Olivia?"

"They are planning to do something we are unaware of," replied Jefferson.

Michael and Sam smiled a little and left, they knew perfectly well what *that* meant. But only if they knew about the precautions Oliver had taken to make sure that the FBI couldn't track him or Calvin, they would have realized that the job was much harder than they thought.

Evelyn's apartment:

Rob was staring at the television screen. That was not unnatural. Most of the kids his age loved the TV. The odd thing was what he was watching. He was watching a documentary about astronomy. His sister came into the room and sat down beside her brother. She had just returned from her job at the Grocery store, and needless to say, she was tired.

Evelyn said, "Another documentary about stars? Seriously?"

"Yep, since you won't get me a good telescope, I have to watch these documentaries," said her brother, with his eyes glued to the screen the entire time.

"I told you, Rob, we don't have enough money to spend on those things."

"Oh, please! You are too old, you wouldn't understand."

Evelyn looked at her brother with astonishment. "Old? I'm twenty-five."

"Fourteen years older than me, that's a lot."

"Fine, let's just watch TV."

After a moment of silence, Rob said, "I'm sorry."

"For what?"

"I know we can't afford the telescope, yet I ask for it repeatedly."

Evelyn ruffled her brother's hair and said, "You are my brother, you can ask me for anything."

In that instant, Evelyn made up her mind to do anything that she could to get her brother a telescope. That was the least she could do. They almost never went for a vacation or even went to an amusement park. She knew her brother wanted to, but they couldn't, and then all he asked for was a telescope, she could at least get him that. These were Evelyn's thoughts, on the other hand, her brother was feeling very guilty. He was ashamed of the fact that he could not control the impulse to ask for a telescope and his demand had forced *that expression* on his sister's face. It was the expression that she got when she had to deny his requests due to their shortage of money. It was bad enough that she had to work, even today, and rather than celebrating, he had made matters worse. He hated to see his sister with lines of tension on her forehead and the sadness in her eyes. He knew he had to do something about it.

"Do you know what a group of fish is called?" asked Rob.

"A school," said Evelyn.

"Correct, but do you know what a group of young fishes is called?"

Now Evelyn was baffled. "I don't know, what?"

"A preschool," said Rob and burst out laughing.

Evelyn laughed too, and that sound was as good as music to Rob's ears.

A hotel in NYC:

Calvin was sitting alone in the room. Oliver had told him to stay behind, in case something unexpected happened. He had just told Calvin that he needed to take care of some things and had left. Calvin wanted to go with him, he didn't want there to be anything that he didn't know, but he had no choice. Oliver was the one with the entire plan, he needed him. But that was about to change soon. Very soon. Once they had pulled off the next robbery, their loot would be enough for him to spend his life in luxury. So, Calvin had made a plan of his own. He was going to sell out his partner and take the money for himself. Not the most original of plans, but definitely one of the most beneficial. Calvin was not a man who troubled himself with things like moral code and loyalty, the only thing he cared about was the money he had and the life he was going to lead.

Calvin still remembered the day he had met Oliver. He had been sitting in his run-down apartment when he had received a message from an unidentified number with explicit instructions to go to a café. He had ignored the message, but then he had received another message, this time it said that it was a once-in-a-lifetime choice, and the correct action taken would make him rich enough to not worry about money ever again. That promise changed his mind. He had reached the café at the indicated time and that was where he had met Oliver for the first time.

At first, he had been skeptical as Oliver had told him that he had an idea for a two-man job and all he needed was a crook who could act well. Although Calvin had been quite enraged at being called a crook, he was quite impressed by the man who had managed not only to find him but also get enough information about him so as to know that he had tried his hand at acting before pursuing a career in crime due to financial issues. He had agreed to hear the plan, and when he did, he hadn't hesitated in saying that he was in. The plan was nothing short of brilliant and it was the definition of ingenious. He especially liked the part where he had to impersonate the guard. That was the correct utilization of his acting abilities, which was something he was extremely proud of. But soon he had realized that Oliver was keeping things from him, not telling him the entire plan. In a way, it was good for Oliver, since if he had told Calvin the entire plan, Calvin would not have hesitated in killing him and getting the diamonds just after the completion of the first robbery. He had killed for money before, and he was not one of the people who would hesitate to do it again.

Suddenly, the door of the room opened, and Oliver entered. He said, "Show me the uniforms."

Calvin got up and went to the cupboard in the room and extracted a small bag. Inside were two uniforms. Oliver took them each in his hand and then held them up in the light. He said, "We need new shirts. Cheaper ones. The pants would do, but the shirts would stick out."

Calvin sighed and said, "These look exactly the same."

"Yeah, they do, but when there is direct light on them, which there will be, the quality of cotton is highlighted. The difference in the fabric shows and we don't want that."

Calvin nodded and said, "I'll get it done."

Oliver shook his head and said, "I told you, Calvin, we cannot afford mistakes, the man we are up against is quite good at what he does."

Calvin paused. There was a question which he had always wanted to ask Oliver, but he never had. Now was the time to do it. "What's your beef with the guy anyway?"

Oliver looked at him and his eyes were unusually bright, even from behind his glasses. "That's none of your business. You want the money? You'll get it only if you do what I say."

Calvin was not stupid. He could sense when things were about to get out of hand. "I'll get the shirts done," saying this, he exited the room.

Oliver took off his glasses and ran a hand over his forehead. That was a mistake. He looked at his hand and then ran into the washroom.

Williamson Residence, NYC:

Jack had reached home, and he was now standing in front of his father, who was seated in an armchair facing his son. There was a curious mix of irritation, anger, and concern on the senior Williamson's face.

Harold said, "Do you know what you have done?"

Jack did not reply, he knew exactly what he had done, but he didn't say anything. Now was not the right time.

"You have cost the company a lot of money and you have also made a dent in my reputation of never backing off from my word," said Harold, answering his own question.

Jack was smart, he knew his father was not the kind of person who could stay angry with a person after they realized and accepted their mistake.

"My apologies Dad, but I just wasn't feeling up to it, I believed it would be better if I shifted the meeting to a later date rather than compromise the deal."

Jack was right. His father had not been expecting any apologies, but when he got one, he could not help but let go of his anger.

"It's all right, but from the next time, try to think about the consequences of your action before you take one."

Jack agreed in a responsible manner and left the room. He did not waste even a single moment and went to the garage straight away. He needed to check on the *Animalia*.

CHAPTER FOURTEEN

It was late evening and Jefferson felt sure that the people working on the case were in dire need of rest. Most of them had been overworking themselves and that could affect their performances, which would be unfortunate.

He walked up to where the other four were seated and said, "All of you need to rest, we can work on this tomorrow."

There was no argument from anyone, and Jefferson took this as a sign of the extent of their fatigue. Brandon and Olivia were the first ones to leave for the temporary residence that the FBI had arranged for them. They were followed by Michael and in the end, Sam. Jefferson stayed behind with the intention of going over the case files once more, but after twenty minutes he felt certain that if he did not rest, he would not be able to concentrate on what he was doing and that might become the reason for an oversight on his part. After safely locking away the file in a drawer in his desk, he too left the building and went home.

Buy it All Supermarket, NYC:

Just like everyone, going shopping for groceries was not Michael's Idea of a relaxing evening, but he had no choice. The state of his fridge at home was quite alarming. It was empty, as empty as it had been when he had bought it. He had been putting off the shopping for quite a few days and that had resulted in this forced trip to the supermarket.

Of course, there was the other alternative of eating from a restaurant, but Michael always preferred to eat what he cooked himself, he knew what went in it and the hygiene levels with which it was cooked, something that couldn't be said for the restaurants. One moment he was thinking about what he was buying and the next moment, his mind had wandered. But this time, he was not thinking about the case, this time he was thinking about Evelyn. Try as he might, he could not get her out of his mind. There had been something in her personality, a remarkable calmness, something which Michael's life lacked. While thinking about her, he remembered something. Something that he had seen in her house. A calendar, A date. He looked at his watch. It was just after eight. He hurried out of the supermarket and drove straight to Evelyn's building, stopping just once on the way.

Michael ran a hand through his hair and rang the doorbell. Evelyn opened the door and was surprised to see him. Rob's voice came from within the house, "Who is it?"

Evelyn did not reply, she said, "How may I help you, agent?"

Michael seemed to be nervous, he said, "I'm sorry, but I believe that it's Rob's birthday, I just got a gift for him."

"What?"

Michael held up the gift and Evelyn moved back form the door to let him enter. As he went inside Rob saw him and his eyes widened.

"You!"

"Happy birthday, Rob," said Michael and handed him the package.

Needless to say, the situation was awkward. There was tension in the room which made Michael feel that it was wrong of him to come to the siblings' house. Afterall, he had visited their house under more formal circumstances the previous time and making the shift to an informal visit was not as easy as he had expected. But the tension did not stop Rob from tearing the wrapper of the gift with enthusiasm and when he saw what was inside, he gave a shriek of delight. It was a telescope.

Seeing the gift, Evelyn looked at Michael with wide eyes and said, "How did you know?"

Michael said, "Oh well, when I was here earlier, I sort of happened to look into Rob's room as the door was ajar, I saw a calendar with today's date encircled and birthday written on top of it. It was pretty obvious."

"No," said Evelyn. "I mean how did you know about the telescope?"

Now Michael was getting self-conscious. "That was a bit more complicated. The wallpaper in his room has a beautiful print of stars, and he was even wearing a shirt with stars when I saw him for the first time. In the newspaper rack in your living room, there are some cutouts and books regarding stars, so I made a gamble and bought him a telescope with the idea that he might be interested in star gazing."

Evelyn was just staring at Michael, but Rob said, "Thanks a lot! But you're wrong."

"You don't like star gazing?"

"No, I love it!" said Rob. "But it isn't my birthday, it's hers."

Michael looked at Evelyn who was still staring at him. "I'm going to the window in my room," said Rob and went in. Now the only occupants of the living room were Evelyn and Michael.

Finally, Evelyn seemed to be able to control her tongue once again, she said, "Would you like some coffee?"

"Oh no! I wouldn't want to trouble you," said Michael.

"Not at all," said Evelyn and went into Kitchen.

Once she was gone, Michael let out a sigh. To say the least, the past few minutes had not been the most comfortable ones.

After a moment Evelyn returned with two cups of coffee. Michael had expected the conversation to go as awkward as the previous time, but he was pleasantly surprised. Soon Michael and Evelyn were talking like old friends. Michael found it was easy to talk to Evelyn, while she believed that he was someone who did not judge her on the basis of her financial status.

"It was nice of you to get a gift for Rob."

"But you should have been the one getting the gift, it was your birthday."

Evelyn shook her head and said, "This was the best gift for me."

There was a moment of silence. Then Evelyn said, "So did you solve the case?"

Michael shook his head and said, "Nope, our opponents are quite cunning."

Evelyn said, "Don't worry, you'll get him."

Michael looked at her. "How are you so confident?"

"A man who was smart enough to get the right gift for a child by just looking at his bedroom is smart enough to catch a few crooks."

Michael laughed. It was very rare when someone complimented him in such a manner. The single sentence which Evelyn had just spoken had boosted his confidence.

Michael asked, "So Evelyn, what do you do?"

"A little bit of this, a little bit of that," replied Evelyn sheepishly. "Currently I am helping out at a grocery store, I just earn enough to be able to take care of the bills without taking much from the insurance money. I need that for Rob's education."

Michael looked surprised, and he was about to ask a question, but he didn't. He didn't have to. There was a photograph on a side table in the room. In the photograph, one could clearly make out a younger Evelyn, with a couple who looked so much like her that it was almost impossible to miss the fact that they were her parents. Evelyn was holding her father's hand while her mother held a baby in her arms- Rob. That was the only picture on the side table and as far as Michael could see, the only picture in the entire house. Factoring in the financial condition and the fact that Evelyn was the one taking care of the monetary aspect of Rob's education, it was not too hard to realize that their parents had passed away. Not very long ago, judging by Evelyn's age, as she would not have been allowed to have custody of her brother if she was a minor herself. By now, it was obvious that the insurance money she was referring to came from the life insurance of her parents.

Michael and Evelyn talked for some more time, until Rob came out of his room and said, "I'm going to bed."

Evelyn looked at the clock and realized that it was almost eleven. Michael got up and said, "I've taken up quite a lot of your time."

"It was good to talk to a friend," replied Evelyn.

"Thanks for the gift, Michael," said Rob.

"Don't mention it buddy."

After Michael had left, Evelyn was lost in thought. She didn't even remember the last time she had been able to talk to someone with such ease, without even the slightest trace of hesitation.

It was Rob who put her feelings into words when he said, "I think Michael's cool."

A few floors below, Michael had exited the apartment and was about to sit in his car when a man brushed roughly past him.

"Hey!" exclaimed Michael.

It was a moment before Michael realized that the man had pressed something into the palm of his hand. It was a chit of paper with two words across it – *Hello Again.*

Undisclosed FBI Safehouse:

Brandon and Olivia were sitting in the living room of the small apartment which the FBI had arranged for them, as their temporary residing area. The house itself was scantily furnished, with everything of need but no unnecessary luxuries. There was a kitchen stocked with some vegetables, fruits, and other edibles. All of this was not out of the ordinary, but the feature that distinguished the house from a normal one was that the main door and the windows of the house operated on an ingenious mechanism. There were two guards posted outside the flat at all times, and while the privacy of the couple was respected within the house, they could not open the windows or the door without alerting the guards outside. If they did so, the door would trigger a loud alarm which would result in some agents coming at the ex-cons with guns and handcuffs. The only way to avoid this was to inform the guard of what they were doing via an intercom so that he could momentarily disable the alarm. This setup made Brandon and Olivia feel as though they were still in prison, much better than before, but still a cage.

Brandon said, "So are you going to call her now?"

"No."

"No?"

"You're going to call her."

"Why me?"

"Because people usually think of a male when they hear the word thief, and we want her to believe that you are the one who has threatened to steal her son's collection and working on what's already present in her subconscious will be to our advantage."

For a moment, Brandon seemed to be satisfied but then, after a moment he got a puzzled expression on his face. "How are we going to make the call? All of the calls we make from the phone provided are tracked."

Olivia smiled and took out a small burner phone from her pocket. "Jefferson 'accidentally' left it at the office today and I picked it up. Only he will know about the calls we make from this."

Brandon smiled a little. He had always admired his wife's cleverness, something which had been invaluable to them on countless occasions.

Brandon took the phone and dialed the number. After a moment he said, "Hello Mrs. Williamson."

"Who is this?"

"The man who is going to steal your son's collection."

"What? Who are you?"

"You are not going to get any further introduction than the one you just got, now, if you even think of calling the cops, we will make sure that you and your son don't live to see what happens next."

"Please! Just leave us alone, we can give you as much money as you want!"

"We will get that anyway, *after* we sell your son's collection."

"Please don't take the skins, he loves them."

The Skins. That was something. Brandon said, "Just tell your son to stay away from his collection, we'll steal it tomorrow and we don't want there to be any unnecessary bloodshed."

"*The Animalia* is very well protected, you wouldn't be able to steal it under any circumstances."

In reply, Brandon terminated the call. He looked at his wife. They had something- the *Animalia* and the skins, and that was all they needed.

Williamson Residence, NYC:

Alice was sitting on her bed, trembling. She was thanking God for the fact that her husband was working late and that she was alone in the room otherwise he would have found out about the collection, he would have found out about everything. She wanted to take her husband's help, but she could not. She wanted to call the police, but she could not do anything of that sort. On the other hand, she didn't want to tell her son about the call, but she had to. She got up, put on her dressing gown, and went to her son's room. She knocked on the door and entered.

Jack looked at his mother through sleep-filled eyes and said, "What is it, Mom?"

Alice sat on a chair and said, "Son, first of all, you need to remain calm after hearing what I am about to tell you."

"What? Mom, what are you talking about?"

"I just received a call from the thieves."

That did it. The sleep vanished from Jack's eyes as though it was never there. He was alert and listening to every word his mother was saying. As his mother filled him in on her conversation with the thieves, his anger levels elevated with each sentence. At the end of the narrative, he got up and started pacing the room.

He said, "Enough is enough, they don't know who they are up against, I'll get them!"

"What do you mean?" asked his mother with an alarmed expression.

"I mean that tomorrow I will go to see the collection myself and check the security. If those thieves come for me, I'll take them down."

"Were you listening to a word that I said? They would kill you!"

"Not if I kill them first."

CHAPTER FIFTEEN

The sun rose next morning to find its light being blocked by dark storm clouds that were brewing over NYC. The wind was stronger than usual, and it was evident that the people of the city did not have much time before it started to pour. Jefferson reached the field office to find the rest of the members of his team already assembled. They seemed to be talking about something important and were so engrossed in their discussion that they didn't even notice when Jefferson walked up to where they were sitting.

"Would anyone tell me what's going on?"

Sam, who had tilted his chair on its hind legs, was startled, and he fell down. "What did you watch before coming here today? Batman?" he asked while rubbing the side of his head.

"What is that supposed to mean?"

"That means you need to catch up on pop culture references," said Michael.

Jefferson looked at Michael and what he saw troubled him. He looked as though he had not been able to sleep the entire night. Jefferson did not say anything, but he knew what Michael's problem was. Alcohol Withdrawal. That was the problem, but at times, expressing sympathy weakens the person and thus, Jefferson decided to put up a façade of being oblivious to Michael's symptoms.

Brandon said, "Now that you are here, we need to repeat the entire thing again, couldn't you have come a bit earlier?"

"I'm not late."

Michael sighed and said, "That's as good as stating Einstein- Time is relative."

Jefferson sat down on a chair. "All right, Olivia, did you guys do what I asked you not to?"

Brandon nodded and said, "I have a strong feeling that Jack Williamson will be going to inspect his collection today."

"And better yet, we know what he collects," said Olivia with a cunning smile on her lips.

"How?"

"Someone called his mother, who let slip two words – *The Animalia*, and the skins," began Brandon.

"And Animalia being the Latin for Animals, and skins most probably referring to animal skins, we believe that he collects animal skins," concluded Olivia.

"That's it!" exclaimed Jefferson "That's why he wants to keep the collection a secret, he acquires animal skins and other wildlife-related objects illegally."

"That makes sense. His father would not approve of such a collection, thus, he doesn't tell him and illegally buys it with money from his account," said Michael.

"But he cannot let anyone trace it and thus the discrepancies in the account," said Sam.

Olivia made a mock applause and said, "Finally, all of you are able to catch on!"

Jefferson said, "But why would he go to examine his collection today?"

Brandon adjusted the cuff of his shirt and said, "Well, the person who called him, we don't know who, must have told his mother that his collection would be stolen today. Obviously, his mother would have told him, and her son would go to check the security."

Jefferson stood up and said, "No time to waste then. Michael, you and Sam will come with me, and Brandon and Olivia will stay here."

"Why?" asked Brandon.

"Because we think that you might try to escape custody, so we prefer to reduce the time you spend outside your apartment and the federal building."

Olivia rolled her eyes but did not say anything, Brandon scowled at Jefferson, got up and stormed off.

"Where do you think you're going?" asked Jefferson.

"To the bathroom!" bellowed Brandon.

The three agents got up and were soon on their way to the Williamson residence. The car they had chosen had no visible markings which classified it as a federal vehicle and thus it was ideal for following a suspect.

Jefferson was the one behind the wheel and Michael was riding shotgun. Sam had reached the car just two seconds after Michael and thus, he had been forced to sit in the back.

Sam said, "What is the guarantee that he hasn't already left?"

"He is a spoilt rich kid which means he is in the habit of getting up when people are expected to be at work. Even in times of distress, it is hard to let go of old habits," replied Jefferson.

The rest of the trip went without another word being exchanged between the agents. Each one of them was absorbed in their own thoughts. Finally, they reached a spot near the Williamson residence. They parked on the opposite side of the road, close enough to monitor the activity, but far enough to not be noticed.

"He's got *some* security," remarked Sam.

"That's right. This place has more CCTV cameras than a museum," said Michael.

Jefferson brought out a pair of binoculars and looked in the window of one of the rooms, then the other. He saw Jack, who looked as though he had just gotten up from bed.

Jefferson looked at his watch and said, "It might be some time before he leaves, be prepared to wait."

Indeed, they had to wait for quite some time. But even though the wait was long, the three agents watched the house as eagles watched their prey. Their eyes never left their mark and their concentration never faltered.

After two hours, their wait was over. They saw Jack exit the house and get into his car. Jefferson started the engine but did not move. He let Jack gain a substantial lead before he began his pursuit. Jefferson was an expert driver, and he tailed the car expertly, always a perfect distance away. Michael was assisting Jefferson in keeping an eye on the vehicle, while Sam was keeping a close tab on the route they were following. After Jack had driven the car quite some distance away, he drove into a garage. Jefferson parked the car and waited for him to exit, but nothing happened.

Michael said, "Don't expect to see him come out in the same car."

"What do you mean?" asked Jefferson.

"I mean that he is rich, there is no way he would resort to getting his car fixed in such a garage. He is on his way to view an illegal collection, he would never use the car which everyone knows he owns."

Sure enough. After five minutes, Jack exited the garage sitting in a different car, a car that no one would even imagine that he would care to drive. Jefferson also started the car and soon, the game of cat and mouse had resumed. After travelling continuously for a considerable distance, Jack turned into the lane where some of the most expensive houses were located. The Williamsons owned one of these houses, the one at the end of the lane, which had a private garden and complete privacy. This house was mainly used for parties and other social engagements, as Harold was against the idea of letting a horde of people into the house where he lived, just for the sake of a party.

Jefferson parked the car some distance away and the three agents got out. Jack also exited the car and could be clearly seen conversing with a guard, then handing him the keys to his car and entering the house.

Jefferson said, "Time to catch the man red-handed."

The three agents waited for a few minutes before boldly walking up to the main gate.

The guard looked at Jefferson and said, "Who're you?"

"The man who will make sure that you spend the rest of your life behind bars if you don't open the gate right now," said Jefferson.

Jefferson flashed his badge and the guard looked at someone on the other side of the gate, said something inaudible, and then let the three agents in. Thinking that things went easier than they expected, Michael entered the house and instantly realized what was going on. Two guards had surrounded the agents at their six and two were standing at their twelve. Their muscles flexing and their intentions unsavory. Before the agents could get their guns, the guards were on them. Jefferson presented the guard right in front of him with an excellent example of his right hook, while Sam tumbled on the ground with another. Michael had caught the wild blow of the guard in mid-air, he had then sidestepped, twisting the man's arm with him and then a clean yet powerful strike aimed at the larynx sent the man into the ground. Before the fourth guard could get to him, Michael had his gun in his hands, aiming it right between the eyes of the guard. The guard froze and Michael saw that the other guards were reeling on the ground and Jefferson and Sam were straightening their clothes.

Jefferson turned to one of the guards and said, "Take us to Jack, immediately."

The words had just escaped the man's lips when Michael saw a figure dart out of the house towards the back. Without waiting to explain what he was doing, Michael followed the figure. He was running at a breakneck speed, taking deep breaths, while keeping his mind focused. His feet touched the ground and rose a split second later. It became a perfect rhythm. Soon, Michael had pushed Jack Williamson, made him lose his balance and pinned him to the ground. Jefferson and Sam came running behind him.

"Good job, Usain Bolt!" complemented Sam.

Jefferson leant and cuffed Jack. The Millionaire's son was seething.

"You have no right to detain me!"

"We know about the *Animalia,*" said Michael.

Jack looked at him with a startled expression and let himself be pushed to move towards the gate. The guards were looking at the agents with terror-filled eyes and gave them a clear berth. Jefferson made Jack sit in the back of their car and started the engine with a triumphant smile.

FBI Field Office, NYC:

Brandon was sitting in a chair, thinking, while his wife was tossing a coin in the air with one hand and then catching it with the other. Suddenly, a thought came into her mind.

"We never asked about Claire," she said.

"I did," replied Brandon with a grim expression on his face.

"How is she?" asked Olivia.

Her husband did not reply. She looked at him and said, "Brandon, how is Claire?"

"She...passed away," replied her husband.

"What?" Olivia was thunderstruck. "Who told you?"

"Jefferson did, I asked him when he came to offer me the deal."

Olivia was silent. That was unusual, but given the circumstances, it was perfectly natural. Claire had been a pillar for them, a person they relied on, and a person who had been sentenced to imprisonment with them.

"What about her son?" asked Olivia.

Now Brandon had a look of astonishment on his face which soon turned to one of shame. He said, "I didn't ask about him."

"How could you forget?"

"I was shocked! I had never even imagined that she would pass away in jail, it's a horrible thing to happen to anyone."

"Even more horrible when you have a kid outside," said Olivia in a heavy voice.

For some minutes there was silence. The two people were lost in thought and for the second time in her adult life, Olivia came close to tears. The first time she had done so was when her life had been turned upside down, when she had been arrested and sentenced.

The silence was pierced by the return of the three federal agents. The person who was in their custody was a high-profile individual whose parents were sure to arrive with a bunch of fancy lawyers soon. This meant that the window during which the suspect could be interrogated was closing fast and Jefferson intended to make use of every single minute he had.

Jack Williamson was made to sit in the FBI interrogation room, while Jefferson waited outside. While he was aware of the shortage of time, he also knew that people talked when they were nervous and what better way to achieve that condition than to leave the man alone in the interrogation room. The first thing they did was think about how bad the mess is, then they would increase the stress on their brain by thinking what if they couldn't get out? That was usually when they started to show the first signs of nervousness, the rubbing of hands, the tapping of the table and the perspiration. Next came the thought of why they were alone, why they had been read their rights and made to sit alone in a room facing a mirror, which they knew was a mirror only from their side. That was when they realized that they were being watched the whole time, that someone was viewing them when they were vulnerable, and that realization made a person uncomfortable. That was when Agent Jefferson stepped into the interrogation room.

Jack looked up and said, "You don't have anything to hold me."

"I think we both know that's not true. You know as well as I do why you were there, you were there to check on the Animalia, your collection...sorry, your *illegal* collection of animal skins which even your father is unaware of."

"Do you know who you are talking to? I own cars which are more expensive than your entire year's salary."

"Be that as it may, you're the one in handcuffs."

Jack fell silent. Jefferson said, "There is something I must tell you though, you're lucky."

"How so?" asked Jack sarcastically.

"Because your illegal activities have been discovered at a time when they could be of some use and thus you may have a chance of getting a sentence that is not very severe."

Jack's eyes lit up. If he could just wrap the whole thing without his father knowing...

"How much do you want?"

"If you offer me a bribe again, I will make sure that you never get out of a prison cell."

"Then what do you want?"

"Your cooperation. As you are aware, some thieves have claimed to steal some items from your collection, and naturally, we hope to catch them."

Jack shook his head and said, "If you want to catch them you just missed your chance, they had said that they would be coming for the collection today."

"No thief would be naïve enough to go for the collection after all the activity which has taken place at the property, that too in the presence of federal agents. No, they would now strike at some other time, and we need to be ready."

Jack was confused. "And exactly how do you want me to help you?"

"Tell us everything about your collection, the security arrangements, the contents, everything. Then do what you are told."

Jack nodded like an obedient child.

Central Park:

Calvin was sitting on a bench. The people around him were unaware of the fact that there was a thief in their presence, a thief who was soon going to pull off another robbery. In fact, only two days were left now, then the plan would be almost complete. The completion of the plan meant two things – money would no longer be a problem and he wouldn't need his partner anymore. Calvin snickered. He had always wanted to be a millionaire, who didn't? but then, most weren't bold enough to take the steps that were required to achieve their goal. Calvin was not going to hesitate. He was so close to achieving his life's goal that there was nothing that could stop him. Oliver was not with Calvin; he was in the hotel room. They changed hotels every day, and each time they attempted to move as far away as possible from the previous one, they used fake IDs which were as good as originals, and they had almost no interaction with anyone else. It was Oliver's idea, so that they did not leave a trail or get noticed, but Calvin thought that it was a useless tactic, even if someone did notice them, they didn't have "thieves" written across their foreheads.

Suddenly, Calvin saw a man standing some distance away. He could not be sure, but he felt the odd tingle on his spine which one feels when being stared at. After ignoring the man for a few seconds, Calvin got up and then walked for some time before sitting down on another bench. He looked around him once again. There was no one who was staring at him. He relaxed and laid back on the bench. He told himself that he was panicking unnecessarily, there was no way that the FBI or anyone else could know who he was or what he was up to. He didn't like Oliver, but that didn't mean there was something wrong with his plan, it was perfect, and there were no loose ends that the FBI could take advantage of.

If only Calvin knew how wrong he was, he would have been more careful, because the FBI had already started their search for the man.

Williamson Residence:

Harold Williamson was sitting in his room. He was alone and the door was locked. His head was throbbing with pain, which was obviously due to shock and stress. His wife had just told him the truth about their son, about his collection. He had been a law-abiding man his entire life, never had he thought that his son would turn out to be a criminal. He was further troubled by the thought that even his wife had hidden the truth from him just because she had loved her son. If the robbers hadn't made a threat on Jack's life, then Harold was sure that she would have never told him about the collection.

Harold pulled himself together. This was not a time to feel hurt or angry, this was a time to protect his son. No matter what he had done, he was his son, and it was a father's duty to protect their child. Harold knew that what his son had done had earned him a punishment, but he didn't deserve to die. He picked up his phone and just as he was about to dial a number, he heard a knock on the door. He got up and opened the door to see himself facing his wife.

Alice was in tears. Her eyes were puffy, and her lips were trembling. "Please Harold, do something!"

"He is my son too. I won't let anything happen to him."

"Does that mean you forgive him?"

"That means I can't bear to think that his life is in danger, but in no way does that mean he is getting away with what he has done."

Alice nodded her head. She was ready to accept anything as long as she knew that her son was safe, that he was alive.

Harold was dialing a number on his phone when he received a call from an unknown number. He put the phone to his ear and said, "This is Harold Williamson."

"Hello Mr. Williamson, this is agent Jefferson Brown from the FBI."

CHAPTER SIXTEEN

Michael and Sam were patiently waiting for the drama to begin. Jefferson had called up Jack's parents and that meant it was only a matter of time before things got interesting. True enough, within the hour, Mr. Williamson and his wife were entering the building accompanied by two lawyers. Jefferson greeted the couple and asked them to send the lawyers away at once.

"Are you denying my son the right to engage a lawyer of his choice?" asked Harold.

"No, Mr. Williamson, what I mean to say is that your son will not be needing a lawyer."

"What do you mean?"

"I mean that he is an adult and thus, upon his arrest, he has already agreed to a deal."

"What sort of deal?"

"The sort that exempts him from charges in exchange for his cooperation...and yours."

Mrs. Williamson was about to say something, but her husband signaled her not to. He understood that the agent had something in mind and if the lawyers' presence did more harm than damage, it was better to send them away. After the lawyers had been excused, Jefferson led the couple to a conference room where their son was seated, along with Brandon, Olivia, Michael, and Sam. Alice rushed to hug her son while Harold took a seat, opposite to his son. Michael noticed this but he did not say anything, if anything, he was impressed. Even in such times, the father was infuriated by the actions of his son.

"As I just said, your son has accepted a deal..." began Jefferson.

Harold cut in, "What are the exact terms of the deal?"

"The terms are quite simple, the FBI is in pursuit of the thieves who have claimed that they will be robbing your son's collection soon, to catch them we will need your complete cooperation."

"And our son will go free?"

"He will have to turn in his entire collection, and pay a fine but yes, if everything goes as planned, we will not be pressing any additional charges."

"But the thieves had claimed to rob the collection today."

"After all that happened at the property, it is obvious that they will be choosing another date."

"What happened at the property?"

Jefferson gave him a short but precise description of the events which culminated in Jack Williamson's arrest. Harold listened intently, shooting angry glances at his son occasionally, while his wife's head was bowed with shame at the actions of her son.

"...So, you see, the thieves don't want to attract attention while they are committing the crime, and thus, what happened today ensured that the collection is safe, at least for now," concluded Jefferson.

Brandon smiled slightly. The story and logic that Jefferson had fed the family were far from perfect, but it appeared that they had bought it.

Suddenly, Jack looked up and said, "How did you know that I would be going to the property today?"

Olivia looked at Jefferson with a raised eyebrow. Finally, the kid had asked the right question, the one no one had an answer to.

Jefferson dealt with the situation in a diplomatic manner. "We don't wish to reveal our method of operation, I hope you will understand that Mr. Williamson."

Harold nodded his head thoughtfully. "So, what sort of cooperation are we talking about?"

"Well, first we will need all the information about the contents of the collection and the specs of the vault where it is stored," said Olivia.

"And then we will need to know what is so special about the date that the thieves have chosen," put in Michael.

"The former question has a rather long answer, however, the latter is easily answered. We have a party on that date, at the same venue where my son hosts his collection," explained Harold.

"Safety in numbers," muttered Sam.

"Do you want us to cancel the party?" asked Jack.

"No, we don't do anything out of the ordinary," said Jefferson. "Try to keep everything as normal as possible."

"But that puts us in a position of a major disadvantage," said Brandon. "A party means more people, people that act as a camouflage."

"Not if some of the guests are our agents," said Jefferson. "We'll put up extra surveillance and scrutinize every single person on the guest list. They won't escape this time."

After discussing a few more points of interest, Jefferson allowed Jack to go back home along with his parents. Once Brandon, Olivia and Jefferson were the only ones in the room, the couple decided to touch a point that was quite personal.

Olivia said, "Jefferson, we need to talk."

"About what?"

"About Claire."

"I already told Brandon. He can fill you in."

Brandon cut in and said, "You never told me the entire thing."

"Don't talk in riddles, what do you mean?"

"What he means to say is that what happened to Claire's son?"

"That does not concern you."

"Oh! I think it does, seeing as we were his godparents," said Olivia.

"You were imprisoned, so was his biological mother, his custody was given to his maternal Grandmother."

"Where is he now? Still with his grandmother?" asked Brandon.

"We don't know. After his grandmother passed away, he completely dropped off the grid, ran away and was never seen again."

"You never even tried to find him?"

"We tried but there was nothing much that we could do. His grandmother didn't believe much in education and thus, there was not much to go on from any educational institutes, he never had any of his own bank accounts so nothing there either. Basically, the kid's a ghost now."

"If he's alive," muttered Olivia with a dark expression on her face.

"I don't blame myself for the choices the kid made, nor can you. He could have had a good future, but he threw it all away," Saying this, Jefferson walked out the door, leaving behind two genuinely concerned individuals.

Michael's Apartment:

Michael was thinking. He was pacing the length of his living room and his grey cells were hard at work. Jefferson had said that they only had two days now. Which meant that they had to start laying the trap from the very next day. It would be a complicated process, one that had to be carried out with utmost precision. But that was not the problem, the problem was predicting what move would their opponents make.

Michael could not stop his mind from thinking about the matter at hand, no matter how troubled he felt. Usually, he would take a drink to relax himself, but now that was a sin. In no time at all Michael realized that he was thinking about Evelyn. He wanted to pay her a visit but felt a little self-conscious, he did not want to seem like a stalker. To divert his attention, Michael decided to visit the public library. He loved reading, ever since he was a child, he found that reading was one of the few things that had the ability to rejuvenate him from within.

Just as Michael reached the library, it started to rain. The downpour was quite heavy, and Michael was glad that he had reached his destination before the drops from the sky landed on him. Michael went in and began browsing books. He had just found an interesting novel to thumb through when he saw the entrance of the library open once again. He could not believe what he was seeing. The woman who had entered was none other than Evelyn, and this development left Michael stunned. He found himself staring at her as she went to the bookshelf to get a book. He quickly averted his gaze and tried to focus on his novel as he didn't want to invade her privacy.

But apparently, Evelyn had other plans. She had seen Michael and walking up to him she whispered, "Michael?"

Michael looked at her and then with a look of surprise, he said, "Evelyn? This is a pleasant surprise!"

Michael and Evelyn were soon talking in whispers. They kept their volume very low so as to not disturb the other readers, but they couldn't help but talk to each other. As it turned out, Rob was at a friend's house and thus Evelyn had some free time which she decided to devote to reading. The topics of the conversation between Michael and Evelyn varied greatly, novels, authors, and other forms of literature were the main contributors to the same. They also touched upon the topic of Michael's case but only briefly. After forty minutes of whispering, both of them realized that it had stopped raining. They replaced their respective novels on the shelves and were soon walking on the sidewalk and enjoying the cool air.

"So, you might be close to catching the thieves?"

"We hope so, things have been going quite well, we do have a lead."

"Which is?"

"I'm sorry but I can't tell you that," said Michael with an apologetic expression.

Evelyn nodded and said, "Of course. I understand. Anyway, it was nice meeting you."

"The pleasure was all mine," said Michael.

After Evelyn had gone her way, Michael found himself to be considerably relaxed. His mind was at peace and when he started thinking, an idea came into his mind, which shocked him into realizing what the robbers' next move would be.

Jefferson's apartment:

Jefferson was studying the plans of the location where Jack kept his collection. Indeed, it was quite cleverly concealed. He had constructed a sort of hidden safe in the parking space which was situated below ground level. But now that he had begun to think of ways the property could be infiltrated, he realized that there were multiple ways, especially when a party was in full swing. Anybody could head down to the garage unnoticed, but opening the safe would be quite a task. It required an eight-digit code and as if that wasn't enough, the door had a puzzle-like mechanism for opening it. Everything went well if the code was put in and the puzzle solved within ninety seconds, if not, then an alarm rang out, and the door of the safe was electrified for fifteen minutes.

Jefferson was satisfied with the security arrangements, but then, he had been satisfied in the case of *Les Morceaux de Lumiere* as well. When his wife entered the room, he did not even realize it, but his daughter was not someone who could be ignored. As soon as she stepped into the room, she went straight to her father and sat down beside him.

"Dad, what are you working on?"

"Nothing much, Penny, just trying to catch a robber."

"There are other ways to do that."

Jefferson looked at his daughter and then at his wife. The latter was smiling but she did not say anything.

"What other ways?"

"In a game! Dad, you promised we'd play today!"

"Did I?" asked Jefferson with a deliberately made faraway expression on his face.

"Mom!" said Penny in a threatening tone.

Jefferson laughed and said, "All right, your threats are even worse than what I face at work! Go get the game, I'll clear the table."

Penny jumped to her feet with a wide smile on her face and rushed to her room to get the game. Martha got up to help her husband clear the table. Just as Jefferson finished, his phone rang. The call was from Michael.

"Hello Michael!" said Jefferson cheerfully.

Michael's voice was urgent when he said, "Jefferson, I need you to listen very carefully."

Undisclosed FBI Safehouse:

Brandon and Olivia were in visibly low spirits today. They had not even changed their clothes, nor had they bothered to cook something or even switch on the TV. Their minds were thinking about the same thing, and each was aware of the other's cause of concern.

"Do you think he would be fine?" asked Brandon.

"Of course, his mother was a survivor, and so was he," said Olivia in a definitive manner, although her tone made it feel as though she was trying to convince herself rather than her husband.

"And what about him?" asked Brandon.

Olivia did not reply, this single question had been pestering her for ages and hearing it from her husband only made matters worse. She got up and said, "I'm going to take a shower."

Brandon looked at his wife disappear into the bathroom, and he shook his head sorrowfully.

The next day everyone met early and there were two major reasons for the same. The first was what Michael had told them via a call. He had a theory and that was one which made perfect sense and made matters even more complicated. The second one was that no one could be patient now, with the robbery date so close.

Michael believed that there was no thief who would go to a party when his name was on the guest list and the simplest way to gain access to the premises, without being treated as a guest, was to arrive as a part of the staff. The party was being organized in celebration of the recent acquisition that Harold's company had made. They had taken over a competitor's company and all the business partners had been invited to enjoy the evening with the Williamsons in celebration of the same. As per Jefferson's instructions, everything had to be as normal as possible and thus they could not cancel the party without alerting the thieves, but if they went along with the party then they reduced the chances of ever catching the robbers.

Sam voiced the same when he said, "There is no other option, we have to call off the party."

"Or we can change the venue," suggested Olivia.

Jefferson shook his head. "We cannot do anything of that sort. They acted in overconfidence when they told us their next target, but they aren't stupid, they won't even attempt to pull off the heist if they sense something is off."

"So, what do we do? Just interrogate each and every staff member before we let them in?" asked Brandon.

"No," replied Jefferson "We issue each member of the staff with a GPS tracker, nothing too fancy, just basic live time location tracking."

"And how would that help us?" asked Michael.

Jefferson was about to reply when Sam said, "We can encode them similar to a tracking anklet, if anyone ventures near the area where the safe is located, we'll get an alert, and we will be there."

Everyone thought that the idea was the best one they had at the moment, and thus the arrangements were made for the staff to wear GPS tracking devices at all times.

The next thirty-six hours were one of the most hectic. They worked tirelessly to arrange the security of the place and that too, in a manner that concealed their true purpose. This was done by putting up the surveillance devices at the same time when the property was being decorated. Resting was a luxury that no one could afford and soon the trap was laid. There were cameras at every entrance and there were security guards at every corner, the GPS trackers had been arranged and were kept in boxes in the corner of the storeroom of the property.

In the afternoon, Jefferson was standing near the coffee machine in the bureau when Michael came into his field of vision. He came over to where Jefferson was standing, took a cup and filled it with black coffee.

Michael looked at Jefferson and said, "Tonight is the night."

"Yep, tonight is the night we catch them."

CHAPTER EIGHTEEN

(I)

Oliver was standing in the middle of a long queue. He had slicked his hair back with the help of gel and ditched his glasses for colored contact lenses. He was looking around sharply and spotted Michael at once, he was standing at the entrance of the back gate, from where the staff was supposed to enter. He could be seen instructing the guard to attach something to the ankles of the staff. This was unexpected, and Oliver hated surprises. The moment he saw that the device being attached to the ankles of the staff was a GPS tracker, he felt his pulse quicken. This was an unforeseen obstacle, to say the least, and he did not have much time to think of a way around it. The queue was moving at a good pace, and it would not be long before Oliver's turn would arrive. Every moment was crucial and being stuck in the middle of a large group of people made it difficult to do anything unobserved. Oliver looked around him with a desperate scan and saw nothing that could help him. He was very close to the entrance now and that meant he had a clear view of the device being attached to the staff's ankles. Oliver cursed under his breath. It was one of the trackers that would send a signal to the feds if they were taken off before being deactivated.

Oliver had no option but to resort to causing the one thing that he hated the most – chaos. Chaos was one of the things that were not difficult to achieve, but controlling it was a task that required effort. But it had to be done discreetly, Oliver did not want to attract attention to himself. He looked at the man in front of him, he was tall and buff, the two qualities which almost certainly guaranteed a fiery temper, something that would be very useful in the situation. Oliver braced himself and after a moment, he hurled himself straight towards the man in front of him. The series of events which followed can be explained best by calling them a domino effect. The first man was hurled towards the man in front of him and so on. Very soon there were a lot of impolite words being spoken and some sleeves were being folded. The man who had been pushed by Oliver turned with a menacing expression on his face, but he saw himself staring at Oliver's back.

"What do you think you are doing, huh?" shouted Oliver at the man behind him and gave him a rough push.

The man, enraged by the manhandling, took a wild swing at Oliver's face, which was exactly what Oliver wanted. He ducked at the last moment and thus, the punch, which was aimed at his nose, smashed against the jawbone of the man standing in front of him. Oliver conveniently excused himself from the line just as Michael began trying to control the commotion. As soon as Michael and the guard abandoned their respective posts to separate people from each other, Oliver walked briskly up to the gate, blocked a wild punch that was aimed his way, and avoiding the field of the camera by sticking to the wall on one side of the gate, he entered the property. The game had begun with a bang.

(II)

Jefferson was viewing the commotion on the monitor in front of him. He was seated in a van parked near the house

143

and the moment he had turned his attention to the cameras which faced towards the staff entrance, the first thing he saw was the live demonstration of a fistfight.

"Sam! Go over to the back gate and help Michael," he instructed through the Bluetooth earpiece.

"Copy that," said Sam and rushed towards the back gate.

The two agents and five guards soon managed to calm the crowd enough to warn them that if they didn't watch their behavior, they would get into a lot of trouble. The threat had little effect and the men decided to act like civilized people only when Michael shouted at the top of his lungs that none of them would be getting a penny for the job if they didn't stop.

Sam said, "What a start to a party!"

"Yeah right," said Michael and quickly began sending the staff members in.

Michael had doubled the speed with which the staff was processed, this was because valuable time had already been wasted in trying to regain order and the first guests would soon start arriving.

Twenty minutes later, the first luxury car pulled up on the porch and the party began. Melodious tunes could be heard coming from the direction of the live orchestra and the laughter and chatter of people mixed remarkably well with the same. The party was very well organized, but it was a shame that none of the agents were able to enjoy it. But that was not what could be said for the ex-cons, they were doing justice to the splendid champagne and finger-licking starters.

"Jefferson," came Brandon's voice in Jefferson's ear.

"What is it Brandon, do you see anything?"

"Have you tried the champagne yet?"

"What?"

"It's excellent!"

"Focus on the job."

Michael and Sam were trying to keep as sharp an eye on the crowd as possible. Every time someone even went in the general direction of the safe, they tensed, but then relaxed when they saw that the person's intentions were not menacing.

A waiter came up to Sam with champagne. "Sir, would you like a glass of champagne?"

"No thanks."

"I insist, sir."

After giving the waiter an odd look, Sam refused. The waiter then proceeded to move towards the table where Olivia and Brandon were seated and placed drinks on their table.

Michael was having a tough time concentrating on the job with glasses full of champagne being offered to him, but then he saw Sam staring at him and found the courage to resist. On the other hand, Jefferson, who was seated in the van, was having a hard time trying to monitor all the guests, even with the help of two additional agents.

The only people who were glad of the presence of the FBI agents were the Williamsons. For the first time since the thieves had arrived in their lives, they felt safe. At least until Harold's phone vibrated and he took it out of his pocket. One look at the display confirmed his suspicion that something was wrong, very wrong.

(III)

Calvin was not at the party, in fact, he was quite far away from the venue of the same. While his partner was busy serving drinks to guests, Calvin was sitting in a car and eating a sandwich. The sandwich was not great, but Calvin was hungry, so, at that moment, the sandwich was delicious. Calvin looked at his watch and then looked out of the window. Oliver had given him explicit instructions not to act until the right time. Had it not been a matter of money, Calvin would not have listened to a word that Oliver said, the reason for the same was the short notice on which Oliver had informed him of the change of plans. Initially, he had been under the assumption that they would be robbing the collection together, but then Oliver had given him a separate assignment, one that he had in mind from the very beginning but was a surprise for his partner.

Calvin crumpled the plastic wrapper in which his sandwich was packed and looked at the watch once again. Soon. He then leaned back and took a black bag pack from the back seat. The bag contained something which surprised Calvin even more than the change of plans. Just before he had departed, Oliver had handed him the bag. Upon opening the bag, Calvin saw that the contents were none other than a gun and an extra magazine for the same. When Calvin had expressed his surprise, Oliver had just told him that he might need it.

Now, taking the gun in his hands, Calvin checked the lock, the magazine, and the firing mechanism. The gun was in top condition, there was no doubt about that. Calvin was not an expert with guns, but experience had taught him how to fire and reload, and that was enough.

Calvin looked at his watch one last time before opening the door of the car and stepping out of the car. He ran a swift eye on either side of his car before he looked at his target – The Williamson Residence.

(IV)

Oliver was standing patiently and scrutinizing his surroundings. There were no rules against enjoying a little while working and he had indeed enjoyed himself when he had offered drinks to Sam. He was staring at Brandon and Olivia as though he had seen them for the very first time, which was true to a certain extent. This was the very first time that he had seen the thieves in person. Suddenly he saw Harold Williamson pull out his phone from his pocket and give it a look. Immediately, Oliver saw the businessman's expression change. Tension was visible on his face, and he looked around him with an air of desperation. It was obvious who he was searching for. Oliver knew exactly what was going on and he was ready and willing to play his part in it.

(V)

Harold's hands were shaking. He had just received a message, a message that shook him from within. He was frantically searching for the FBI agents when he saw one of them. Michael was standing a little distance away with his back turned towards the businessman. Harold briskly walked up to him, weaving through the guests expertly and courteously. He tapped Michael sharply on the shoulder and the latter instantly turned around.

"What is it, Mr. Williamson?"

"Look at this," said Harold turning the display of his expensive smartphone towards the agent.

Michael's eyes widened. He began speaking urgently into his microphone and an instant later, the family and Michael were standing outside the surveillance van with Jefferson.

"What was so important that you risked exposing the entire operation?" asked Jefferson.

"There is no operation to expose, we've been deceived."

"What do you mean?"

Michael showed him the message which was displayed on the screen:

Hope you're enjoying the party because a surprise
awaits you at home!

"Does it mean what I think it means?" asked Michael.

"Yes! It means that they are going for the designs! We must stop them at all costs!" Harold shouted.

"What designs? It doesn't make any sense," said Michael.

"Yes, it does. Michael, alert Sam and the other two; leave two FBI agents here and the rest come with me. We're heading to the Williamson residence. I'll tell you about the designs on the way. The thieves made a fool out of us."

(VI)

Oliver saw Sam say something to Olivia and Brandon and the three of them left the party in a hurry. Oliver knew exactly where they were going, after all, he was the one who had sent the message. It was easy to see that his words had the desired effect. The agents were under the assumption that they had been fooled and thus, they had panicked. They would soon be speeding their way to the Williamson residence, unaware of Oliver's real intentions.

Oliver kept down the tray which he had been holding and walked over to the entrance of the house. He peeped out from one of the frosted glasses in the designer doorframe and saw Jack exchanging a few quick words with his father. Both of them were agitated and after a minute's conversation, Harold sat in a car and sped off, while Jack lit a cigarette. Oliver heaved a sigh of relief, for a moment it seemed like Jack would also leave the party and that would have created a problem, but seeing that he was staying behind meant that Oliver could proceed with the next part of his plan. He quickly went to the kitchen and exited through the back entrance after showing the guard his pass. He then proceeded to walk briskly towards a sedan parked a block away and sat in it. Opening his laptop, he connected to the network of the CCTVs of the property. With the FBI surveillance Van no longer on the premises, the two agents and guards were the only ones who stood in Oliver's way. They were a hindrance, but now that the FBI was not actively monitoring the footage, Oliver could hack the cameras.

He typed furiously and for a moment, he felt as though he was typing out his own destiny.

(VII)

Calvin was tip-toeing his way to the upper floor of the house. His mind was alert to even the faintest of sounds and the shadows of movement but so far, he had not faced any trouble. He had been able to get into the house by following the steps that Oliver had laid out for him. It appeared that somehow, he knew everything about the house's security systems and the layout of the guards. He had asked him how he had obtained this information, but Oliver had given him the standard reply – it was none of his business.

Initially Calvin, like the feds, had believed that they were robbing the collection of animal skins and other wildlife-related items but then Oliver had told him that it was a bluff, a diversion to make sure that the FBI didn't get a whiff of their real plans, and it had worked. The FBI, as well as the majority of the guards, had been stationed at the venue of the party and that meant that gaining access to the residence was not much of a challenge. The plan, as Oliver had revealed to Calvin, was to rob the safe in the Williamson residence. The safe had quite a large amount of cash and Jewelry, enough to get them out of the States without having to sell the diamonds. But that was not what they were after. In addition to the money, the safe contained the plans for the latest machines designed by the engineers at one of the companies owned by Harold Williamson. It was stipulated that their company had managed to create a machine, a generator, which created energy with such efficiency that it could power up a small city by using just half the number of resources that were usually required for such a task. It was simple math, if the number of resources required were halved, then the profit would double. Calvin had no interest in the energy business, but even the most foolish person would realize the value of such a design in the black market. The truth was, it had no value, it was up to them to quote any price they wanted.

Calvin had been enraged for being kept in the dark, but now he understood why Oliver had changed the strategy, why he wanted to get the plans and sell them off as soon as possible. He realized that it was the best idea to leave the States forever, they had made quite a stir and, in their profession, remaining anonymous was the greatest prize one could hope for. Although he had been quite surprised how Oliver knew of the designs, as he had not even heard of the invention of any such machine, but he reminded himself that any company would try to keep a breakthrough of this magnitude under wraps until they were sure of the abilities of the creation.

So far everything had gone smoothly, none of the guards had seen him and he had not tripped any alarms, he expected no company. Oliver was keeping an eye on the agents at the party, which meant that if anything went sideways, he would inform his partner at the earliest. Calvin cracked his knuckles in a confident manner, he could easily manage the job at hand, after all, he was cracking safes since he was a kid. Calvin entered the bedroom of the Williamsons and saw the painting which

Oliver had mentioned. According to Oliver, the safe was behind the painting, a safe whose specs had been provided by Oliver. It was not a job that would take a long time, but one that had to be done with caution. He kept his bag on the floor and with his leather-glove clad hands, he moved the painting to one side and saw the safe. But something was wrong, the safe was not the one that Oliver had provided the specifications for, it was different, harder to crack, and impossible using the tools that Calvin had.

Calvin could not understand what was going on, Oliver never made mistakes, but he was staring right at one. Suddenly the faint sound of police sirens reached his ears. He quickly looked out of the window of the room and saw FBI agents exiting cars and rushing towards the house. Now Calvin panicked, the first thought that came to his mind was that he had been betrayed, that Oliver had tricked him. But then he realized that Oliver had given him an escape route in case something went wrong, and it was the very route that Calvin decided to use to get out. He took out a black suit jacket and black pants from his bag and changed with miraculous speed. He could hear the guards and the Feds entering the house and that meant he did not have much time. He stuffed everything else into the bag and clipped his gun to his belt.

Calvin was going to use the biggest advantages he had at the moment – the sense of confusion and the fact that the agents did not know his face, or so he thought. He was going to blend in with the property guards and no one would even know who he was. At first, everything seemed to go well, he ran out of the room and began searching the other rooms and shouting "Clear!" just as the other guards were doing, but then, when he descended the stairs and came into Michael's field of vision he saw a sense of recognition in the man's eyes and that was when he realized that he was doomed.

Michael whipped out his gun and pointing it straight at Calvin, he shouted, "Freeze!"

Calvin did the exact opposite of what he was told. His fiery temper took control and taking his own gun into his hands, he fired a shot aimed towards Michael and ran towards the back exit of the house. Jefferson saw him and he and Sam both fired and missed, but Michael was hot in pursuit of the criminal. He ran towards Calvin, while the latter turned and shot at Michael.

Just as Calvin was about to shoot again, the sound of a single shot rang out in the air and the bullet which had escaped Michael's gun pierced Calvin's heart.

In the last seconds of his life, Calvin realized the truth. He understood why Oliver had changed the plan, why he had given him the gun and why he had told the FBI agents where he was. He realized that Oliver had done to him what he had been planning to do to Oliver all along. Calvin realized that he had been betrayed, just as he closed his eyes for the last time and fell into an endless slumber.

CHAPTER NINETEEN

Oliver was back at the party and his eyes were trained on Jack. Jack was displaying signs of stress and thus, whenever, Oliver offered him a drink he took it and drained the glass at once. This cycle continued quite a number of times before Oliver realized that it was time to do what he had been waiting for. He went near the entrance of the basement and then pressed the button of a remote detonator. Instantly there was a deafening noise as a car parked near the house exploded. Oliver smiled a little as he saw the people run around in confusion. He was the one who had parked the car on the porch of the house, and he was the one who had fitted a remote detonation device near its fuel tank.

Oliver waited for some time before executing his second act. He let the panic reach its pinnacle when he took out his mobile phone, tapped on the screen a few times, and the lights of the entire property went out. He then had to wait for just a moment before the guards at the entrance of the basement abandoned their post to understand what was going on. Seeing his chance, Oliver quickly proceeded towards the safe and then all he had to do was wait. If he knew anything about human nature, he knew that in times of crisis, a person went near their most prized possession in order to guard it and that was what Jack would do.

Oliver had to wait in the shadows only for a few moments before he heard a man descending the stairs and coming towards the pillar that concealed the safe. He saw the outline of Jack's figure and waited patiently as the latter opened the safe. The mechanism of the emergency light was activated and just as that light illuminated Jack's face Oliver took a syringe out of his pocket and injected it into Jack's neck from behind. Within a few seconds, Jack lay crumpled on the floor. Oliver looked at the collection in front of his eyes, took out a foldable bag from under his jacket and began humming a little tune while committing a presumably impossible robbery.

Williamson Residence:

Michael was staring at the body of Calvin. His hands were not shaking nor was he displaying any other signs of distress, but Jefferson knew that from the inside he was trembling. It was a completely natural reaction after killing a person in the line of duty. It was not a murder, but still, taking a person's life was nothing to be taken lightly.

Jefferson looked at Michael and said, "Are you all right Michael?"

"I'm fine. The man was a criminal."

Jefferson did not say anything else. He knew that no matter what happened, Michael would not share his feelings with him. Harold Williamson walked in through the front door and faltered when he saw the body.

"What happened?"

Jefferson looked at Michael and then said, "We stopped a robbery, that's what happened."

At that precise moment, Jefferson's phone rang, the call was from Jack. In a wheezing voice, he said, "Jefferson, they... they stole it."

Jefferson almost dropped the phone from his hands. "What?"

"They stole the collection."

These words were enough to shock Jefferson into realizing the truth. One of the thieves had used his partner as a distraction to make the FBI go away from the real sight of the crime.

"Jefferson, what happened?" asked Michael.

"They got the collection."

Michael and Sam just stared at Jefferson, but Harold's' face went pale and his wife almost fainted. Michael looked as the paramedics took away Calvin's body. The thief had used him as a weapon for murder, to eliminate an unwanted variable from the equation.

"Well, what now?" asked Brandon.

Jefferson did not reply, instead, he walked out of the house and drove away.

The party venue:

Jack was sitting on a chair with a glass of water in his hands. A medic had checked him and given him a clean bill of health, however, Jack felt far from all right. In the course of a single evening, his house had been targeted and his collection had been robbed.

The other guests of the party were still in confusion. The police were trying to take their statements but most of them were absolutely clueless as to what was going on. As far as any of them were concerned, they had arrived at a party, and then a car had blown up, the lights had gone out and what followed was absolute chaos. Then the guards had found Jack lying senseless in the basement and the open door of a seemingly nonexistent, but definitely empty, safe.

Jack had just kept his glass of water on the table when he saw Jefferson's car pull up on the porch. He walked towards the entrance in a hurry and met Jefferson just as he was about to enter the house.

"Did the thieves rob our house too?"

"No, we prevented that," replied Jefferson. "Now, I need you to tell me exactly what happened here."

"What happened was that the thieves knocked me out and stole my collection!"

"I require a more definitive and less informal description of the events. Now sit down and talk."

While Jack relayed the events to Jefferson. Michael went down to check the safe along with Sam and Brandon, while Olivia stayed with Jefferson, listening closely to what Jack was Saying.

Michael reached his destination and inspected the safe without touching it. After a moment he said, "One thing is quite certain, the thief did not break into the safe. It was opened in the usual manner, no signs that the lock has been tampered with."

"And Jack was the only person who could have done that," said Sam.

Brandon was looking at the safe from quite a distance, then he walked very slowly towards Michael, who had his back turned towards him. Brandon flicked Michael on the ear and this action earned him an angry look from Michael.

"Exactly what do you think you are doing?"

"Demonstrating my theory."

"And what is your theory? Flicking a person's ear hurts?"

"No, what I wanted to say was that the robbery was ingeniously carried out. Jack was made to panic and thus the thief knew that he would go to check on the collection, which is why he was waiting for him right where I was standing a minute ago."

Sam said, "So when Jack had opened the safe, the man just had to knock him out and he would have access to the open safe without any trouble. That's smart."

Soon the three men were standing near Jefferson and the five of them were discussing what they had learned so far. The theory formed by Michael, Sam and Brandon was correct and now it was clear how the thief had committed the crime. The only question that remained was to decide what to do next. The thief now possessed what he was after, he had the skins, and he had the diamonds and he had no one he had to share his loot with. Everything seemed to be going well for him, but the conditions were unfavorable for the ones on the side of the law.

After confirming that there was nothing that the agents could find out at the crime scene, they decided to head back to the office. It was late night, but no one wanted to sleep, each one of them was enraged and motivated. They wanted to do all that they could to catch the thief.

They reached the office just after twelve and assembled around the large table that had been set up near the coffee machine. Their tasks were clearly divided. Brandon and Olivia had a map of the area opened in front of them in order to figure out the most probable escape route that would be taken by the thief. Michael and Jefferson were going over the footage of the entire duration of the party to see if they could find anyone suspicious and Sam was tasked with trying to get as much information as possible from Calvin's mobile. For about an hour there was absolute silence as the people worked on their respective tasks devotedly.

Finally, Brandon said, "We've got something."

Everyone stopped what they were doing as all eyes turned towards the couple. Olivia turned the map towards the audience and said, "There are three routes which the thief could have taken to exit the house."

"But the first one of them involved getting out of the front porch and that was ruled out since that was where the guards were concentrated," explained Brandon.

"Now, he could have taken any of the two routes that are left but we believe he took this one," said Olivia tracing a route with her pencil.

"And why is that?" asked Jefferson.

"Because that route has the least number of cameras and also, it originates from the staff exit of the house which was the most convenient place to exit from, especially during the panic," said Olivia.

"All right then, Sam, get the footage from that route."

"On it!"

Michael said, "The thief had hacked into the cameras before he committed the robbery, which means that we have absolutely no footage of that time, and so far, I have not found anyone who sticks out in the footage of the party."

"There is not much on Calvin's phone. Apparently, he had bought a new one recently so that in case someone got hold of it, it wouldn't have much information on it," explained Sam.

"So, there is nothing that can help us?" asked Michael.

"There is something. He had made multiple calls to a number within the last two days."

"And who does the number belong to?" asked Jefferson.

"I'm not sure, he hasn't saved it, I could pull up the records but that would take some time."

Jefferson realized that what they were doing was not very productive. They were working in the heat of the moment without a plan. "All right, pull up the records but get some rest first."

"Jefferson, with all due respect, we cannot rest," said Michael.

"That would not be wise, presently we have nothing to work on, no leads whatsoever," said Jefferson.

What Jefferson had said was correct and everyone knew that, therefore, all of them left the office with the conviction of coming back the next day to get the thief and also get some payback for all the embarrassment he had caused them.

A hotel in central NYC:

Oliver was seated in an armchair in a luxury hotel room. His choice of accommodation after committing a robbery was quite unorthodox but, like everything else he did, there was reason for that as well. Whenever a robbery was committed, the first place that the FBI went to look for the thieves, were small hotels, places where one could stay without being detected, but no one would even think that a man who had committed a robbery, would boldly go ahead and stay in a luxury hotel.

Oliver's fingers were closed around a cup of strong coffee. He needed to clear his head and he found that coffee was best for achieving that result. After he had emptied his cup, he felt a lot better than before. Even though he was tired, he could not help but wonder what would be going through the minds of the players in the opposite team. He figured that they might be thinking that he was done and that he would try to escape but little did they know that was only partially correct. There was no plan which could work perfectly without improvising and thus, as the agents had improvised, so had Oliver. The robberies were no longer the only thing he planned to do, he planned to teach a lesson to the ones who stood in his way.

CHAPTER TWENTY

The next morning, Michael woke up late. Things were different when you had a job to do, leads to chase and clues to piece together, but now they had nothing. Michael had put a bullet in their only lead and the thief had managed to get away with the collection anyway. He was about to take a shower when his phone rang. The call was from Sam.

"What is it, Sam?"

"Where *are* you?"

"I'm just reaching," lied Michael. "Why? What happened?"

"I got a name on the number from Calvin's phone, and you'll be interested to see who it is."

These words were enough to give Michael what he had been lacking in the morning. A purpose. His energy returned and within forty-five minutes, he was entering the building with a cup of coffee in his hand.

As he stepped off the elevator on his floor and went towards the table, he saw that the others were already looking at Sam, who seemed to be explaining something.

Michael said, "Sorry I'm late, there was traffic."

"Apologies later," said Jefferson. "Sam has just found out something very interesting about the number."

"As I was just explaining to the others, the number is not of a specific person, it is a centralized number for a call center."

Michael was puzzled. "A centralized number for what?"

"That is where it gets interesting, it's the number for a top of the line cruise service."

"But why in the world would Calvin call the number for a cruise service?" asked Michael.

This time it was Brandon who spoke. "Well, your question's not original, all of us are wondering the same thing."

Olivia said, "I am still voting that he might be using it to get out of the country."

Jefferson shook his head. "No, a cruise is not very fast nor is it very subtle. It is a pleasure trip, not an escape route."

"Maybe that was what Calvin planned to do after he got his share," suggested Sam.

"No, it was too early to start planning for something he would after getting his share and secondly, why are we guessing? Why don't we just ask the company?" said Michael.

"I tried," said Sam with an irritated expression on his face. "But they say that they have a strict privacy policy and they do not share the details of the conversation they had with a potential customer."

"But this is regarding an investigation!"

"That is exactly what I told them, but even then, they say that it would take time to get the data."

"In other words, they don't want to give it to you," said Olivia.

Jefferson said, "We need to get that data, I'll send over an official order to their place asking for it."

Michael nodded his head with satisfaction. Finally, they had something to work on again.

A Car workshop, NYC:

Oliver was standing outside the entrance of an old car workshop. The condition of the place was such that it appeared to be part of a haunted house rather than a place where cars were fixed. Oliver walked into the garage and saw two mechanics working on a car while another one, a supervisor, was leaning against the wall with his eyes trained on the screen of his phone.

Oliver walked up to the supervisor. "I would like to see the manager."

The man looked at Oliver strangely and said, "What do you want from him?"

"The only thing which he sells, other than his services."

"I don't know what you're talking about."

"I think you do," said Oliver and handed the man a chit of paper.

The man looked at the chit of paper once and then said, "How many?"

"Just one."

"Custom?"

"Standard."

The man nodded and went to an inner room. Oliver remained standing and after a wait of just five minutes, the man came out and handed Oliver a black case. Then he said, "Come back for the vehicle after an hour."

Oliver nodded and after checking the contents of the case to his satisfaction, he handed the man an envelope of cash before walking out of the garage. He had obtained what he needed, now was the time to do what he wanted.

(III)

Michael was feeling hopeful, and it was a wonderful feeling. The shipping company had finally sent them the details regarding the multiple calls Calvin had made and they appeared to be quite relevant. According to the records, the calls had been made under the name Rafool Edmunds and were regarding the various cruises that the company offered. He would call once a day and get the complete information for a cruise and then disconnect, only to call the next day to obtain information for some other. Now, the details for all the cruises he had asked for were laid right in front of the agents and their consultants, but no one could make any connection between them.

Sam picked up a sheet of paper and said, "This one is for the Caribbean, surely this has nothing to do with the robbery?"

"We never know," said Brandon. "Judging by his performance so far, we cannot omit anything."

Olivia nodded. "But as far as I can see, they could be thinking about boarding any one of them and we wouldn't know which one."

"Maybe, but what intrigues me is the fact that he managed to cover his tracks here as well, he never showed his own face, nor did he enquire about just one route. It's like he is providing us with leads just to amuse himself," said Michael.

Brandon yawned and said, "Well, I say we try to rattle our brains tomorrow."

"He may be out of the country by then," said Sam sharply.

"No, he'll stay here," said Olivia.

"And how do you know that?"

This time it was Michael who spoke, he said, "Because if he was asking about the cruises then it is obvious that he plans to leave via the sea route but none of the cruises he has asked for depart less than three days from today."

"So that means he is in the States for at least three more days?" asked Sam.

"Precisely," said Brandon while looking oddly at Michael.

Jefferson said, "It could be a diversion, to make us think that he isn't leaving earlier."

Brandon said, "Maybe, but in that case, we must also assume that he has already left."

"Let's be optimistic," said Sam.

"I agree with the little one," said Olivia.

As the couple got up to leave, Jefferson called them from behind. "I hope you remember what I tell you every day."

"Yes, how can we forget? If we attempt to deviate, even slightly, from the route to temporary residence, you will be on our tail within minutes, and we would be in cuffs and in our respective cells within the hour without any hope of ever getting out," said Olivia.

Jefferson did not give them a second look and then began reading through the papers in front of him. Brandon and Olivia had soon exited the building and were waiting to catch a cab. It was a miracle that Jefferson trusted the duo enough to at least let them communicate via a cab. They did not have to wait long as very soon, a cab halted in front of them, and they got in. The other problem with the living arrangement they currently had was that they could not ask the cab driver to take them to their exact location. They always had to get off two blocks away from where they actually stayed and then walk to their apartment.

Olivia got into the cab and gave the driver their destination. As the driver started the car, Brandon and Olivia were thinking hard. Thinking about what would happen next. About what they would do next.

(IV)

Jefferson was sitting alone in his office. He was trying to figure out which one of the cruises would Oliver board, but so far, he had absolutely no clue. The more he tried to concentrate, the more he got the feeling that there was something unusual going on, that this wasn't just an ordinary robbery, there was more to it than met the eye.

Jefferson got up from his chair and went to pour himself a cup of coffee, but even while he was pouring the black liquid into a cup, he was going over the series of events that had taken place so far. Try as he might, he could find no clue to shed light on the true nature of the matter. His mind was occupied with such thoughts when his phone rang. The call was from one of the guards of the FBI safehouse where Brandon and Olivia were currently living. Lines of worry immediately creased Jefferson's forehead.

"What is it?" asked Jefferson.

"Sir, are they with you?"

"No, haven't they reached yet?"

"No sir, I thought that they were working late."

Jefferson disconnected the call immediately. He knew that something was wrong. He pulled up the live time location from the tracking anklet of Brandon and Olivia. It showed that they were in an old house some distance away. Jefferson was about to leave when an alarm reached his ears, the device had been tampered with. He whirled around towards the monitor to realize that the two trackers had been taken off. Jefferson stood where he was, knowing that by the time he would reach the location, Brandon and Olivia would be long gone.

(V)

Michael was talking with Evelyn. They had exchanged their numbers the last time they had met and tonight, Evelyn had given him a call. It was only after talking for a good half an hour, that they had disconnected the call. At this point in his life, Michael was in dire need of a friend, and he had found that friend in Evelyn. After taking a shower, Michael lay down, but after ten minutes he got up with a groan. He could not sleep, so, he decided to read a book. He had just read a page when his phone rang. Puzzled and not very pleased, Michael received the call and realized that it was Jefferson.

"Hey Jefferson, what's up? Did you get anything?"

"Michael, you need to come back, *now*. And call up Sam too."

"What's the matter?"

"We have a situation."

"What situation? You think the thief would try to escape today?"

"No, but Brandon and Olivia did."

"Did what?"

"They escaped."

"What?" exclaimed Michael in disbelief, but Jefferson had already terminated the call.

Michael hurriedly got dressed and called up Sam.

"Sam, we've got a situation."

"What happened, Jefferson figured out a connection?"

"No, Olivia and Brandon escaped!"

"Oh man! I knew something like this would happen, when?"

"Just some time ago apparently, Jefferson didn't give me the details."

"Now we need to catch two sets of thieves, Brilliant!"

After the call was terminated, Michael exited his apartment and took a cab. He reached the building and Sam caught up with him just as he was stepping into the elevator.

"I can't even imagine how angry Jefferson would be," said Sam

"He is not the only one," replied Michael. "They would have spent all their lives in prison if Jefferson hadn't offered them the deal and this is how they repay him?"

Sam and Michael reached their floor and went straight to Jefferson's office. Jefferson was talking on the phone with someone and motioned the two agents to remain quiet. After a while, he terminated the call and looked at Michael and Sam.

"That was the marshals," he informed them, "They've started looking for those two."

"Where do you think they would go?" asked Sam.

"I don't know, the most obvious answer would be to try and leave the country."

"So that is something that they would not try to do," replied Michael. "They know that they can stay ahead only as long as they don't make obvious moves."

Jefferson nodded and said, "I've called to get the footage from the building exit. I think we'll be able to get something then."

Sam and Michael both took their leave from Jefferson's office and went to their respective desks. While Sam tried to expedite the matter of obtaining the footage, Michael got a list of the places the couple had been to since they had got out of the prison, to see if they could have arranged for a place to hide. It was a long shot, but it was a fact that every human could make mistakes.

After checking the data from the tracking anklet for a while, Michael felt sure that it contained no clue to the whereabouts of the couple. He then decided to check how Sam was doing. In contrast to Michael, Sam had succeeded in his task. He had successfully obtained the required CCTV footage from the cameras located at the exit of the federal building and soon, the three agents were scrutinizing this very footage on the monitor in Jefferson's office.

In the footage, Brandon and Olivia could be clearly seen talking and waiting for a cab. Then a cab stopped for them, they got in and went off. The cab looked like an ordinary NYC cab and Sam immediately noted the number.

"I'll put out an alert for the cab," said Sam and went out in a hurry.

Michael turned to Jefferson and said, "It doesn't make sense."

"What doesn't?"

"Why would they run away? Now that they were helping the FBI, they had a chance of getting their sentence reduced and that way they would have at least been able to live in peace."

"No Michael, it makes perfect sense. I had told them that their sentence would get reduced and not entirely waived off. Secondly, the deal was that if they helped catch the thieves, only then their sentence would have been reduced, and from what has occurred so far, anyone would have thought that it was a lost cause."

"So, you think that if we failed to catch the thieves then they would have worked for nothing?"

"But they were wrong, we are going to catch the thieves, the imitator and the original ones as well."

CHAPTER TWENTY-ONE

No one had slept the entire night. They were working and none of them had even troubled to look at the watch. When the sun rose the next morning, it illuminated three agents who were highly caffeinated and over-exerted. They had managed to find the cab which had been used by the presumed fugitives. It had been left near the last recorded location of Brandon and Olivia, the car had been searched and scoured for any evidence but so far, they had got nothing. The car had been cleaned by alcohol and thus there had been no prints. The DNA evidence had been processed with top priority, but the results were inconclusive. This was nothing surprising since tons of people sat in an NYC cab on a daily basis and thus it was the pot which contained a complex mixture of tons of DNA samples, so much so that not all of it was human.

Suddenly, while working, Jefferson received a message on his mobile.

Hello old "friend"

Jefferson's first thought was to try and trace the connection, but then he remembered that his opponent was not a fool, thus the only thing he did was call Sam and Michael to his office and shut the door.

Michael said, "Why does he always have to pick the wrong time to make contact?"

Sam said, "From his point of view, he always chooses the right time."

Jefferson had started typing a moment ago and now, he sent the message

Don't think this is over, very soon you will be behind bars

Let's keep the incorrect future predictions for later, let's talk business

You want to come in and now you want a deal?

In your dreams

Then what?

I hear that two of your "consultants" are missing.

A chill went down Jefferson's spine. The sentence had a certain feel about it that made it seem like the thief knew more than he was letting on.

That is incorrect. They're in my office, with me

I don't believe that is true

Why not?

Because I'm the one who has kidnapped them

(II)

Oliver was in contact with Jefferson Brown, and he could not help but smile when he imagined the look on Jefferson's face when he realized that his biggest advantage was now in the control of the very person whom he had expected to use the advantage against.

The plan had been made and executed with perfection. Oliver had gone to a garage which was the cover for two operations and one of the operations was providing stolen cars without any registration or any sort of paperwork. The cars were not clean, and that was intentional, the scattered DNA and the dirt and grime reduced the chances of DNA evidence being isolated and the perpetrator being apprehended. After he had managed to secure the couple, he had also wiped the car with alcohol so as to not leave any fingerprints behind. All the registration numbers on the car had been filed off and thus, as far as the government was concerned, the car did not exist.

Oliver terminated the connection and looked around him. He was in an old warehouse in NYC, and it was one of the properties which belonged to some company but due to legal issues, the company could not use it. For the same reason, the property was empty and made a great hiding spot. Brandon and Olivia were in the back of the building and that was where Oliver intended to go now, after all, he had to send a message.

(III)

Jefferson had tried to send messages to the number repeatedly, but he had received no response after the message in which the shocking revelation had been made. In the end, he just gave up with the idea that the connection had been terminated. The three people who were in Jefferson's office looked at each other with serious expressions.

"It appears we were wrong about Brandon and Olivia," said Michael.

"Yes, it appears so," said Jefferson.

"The thief would never do anything without a reason, he must have had one for kidnapping them," deduced Sam.

Michael shook his head. "But that can be anything! From something as simple as removing an obstacle to a complex part of his plan."

Jefferson was silent for a few moments. Then he said, "We need to inform the Marshals, tell them that it is a hostage situation and Brandon and Olivia are not fugitives."

Jefferson picked up the phone in his office and dialed a number. He waited for a few seconds before the call was received and then he proceeded to explain the latest developments in the case in clear and short sentences. When he hung up, his face had an expression of concern.

"What did the Marshals say?" asked Sam.

"That they haven't found any leads so far."

"But that might be because they were looking for places where Brandon and Olivia might hide, not places where they might be kept as hostages," said Michael in a hopeful manner.

Jefferson said, "Let's hope you are right, and the change of perspective does them some good and they get something. Until then, put everything else on hold and try to find some leads as to where they may be."

Jefferson got up and exited the office and entered straight into the office of the head of the unit. Michael and Sam went to their respective cubicles and began their search. After a few moments, the head of the unit came out to address all the agents in the bullpen.

He said, "Everyone listen up! We have a hostage situation and right now the priority is finding where Brandon and Olivia are being kept, so get going everybody!"

The other agents nodded their heads and bustled to get started with the search. For the next hour, security footage was scrutinized, and every other means of surveillance was utilized, but to no avail. The only conclusion which was drawn by everyone was that their adversary was someone who knew how to cover his tracks.

After some time, Jefferson received another message on his phone:

You should watch the news, agent

Jefferson wanted to smash his mobile against the wall. He was fed up with the games, but he had no choice other than to do what he was told. He switched on the television and turned on the news channel, and what he saw almost gave him a heart attack.

He was about to call Michael and Sam when they banged open the door of his office and ran in. They had their phones in their hands it was obvious that they had also received the same message. All three of them had received the same message at the same time, which was an indication of how serious the matter was, but what was even more grave was the fact that the news channel was displaying a live video feed. The presenter was explaining that the feed was from a person who called himself the best thief there was.

"...the man has claimed that he would be removing two people from his path, two people who have been causing him trouble. We warn the viewers, the live feed may contain disturbing imagery," continued the presenter.

The three agents were watching their screens with bated breath. At that moment, nothing existed other than the TV and the office in which they were, and when they saw the live feed, they felt their stomach churn and their hands go cold. Perspiration made their forehead moist and the air around them seemed to get colder.

Brandon and Olivia were sitting down in chairs with their hands tied to the arms and tape across their mouths. A man dressed in black was standing in between the two chairs and he had a mobile in his hand. He typed something and suddenly Jefferson's phone vibrated.

I hope you're seeing me agent

Jefferson did not waste any time, he typed as fast as he could

Don't do this, this is not what you want

The man on the screen laughed. A harsh laugh, that made his two hostages flinch. The man then took out something from the pocket of his jacket and when the agents saw what it was, earth seemed to shake below their very feet. The man had withdrawn a gun from his pocket, and he proceeded to take out the magazine from the other pocket. In front of the eyes of the viewers, he loaded the gun.

Jefferson typed another message:

Please don't do this!

But the man did not even look at his phone. He pointed the gun at Brandon's head and then at Olivia's head. A single shot rang out in the air, everyone's heart seemed to skip a beat and Sam had even closed his eyes, but when he opened them, he saw a very afraid, but still alive couple. The man had shot in the air, but it was enough to strike fear in everyone.

Jefferson was feeling helpless, he was forced to watch the couple's ordeal, but he could not do anything about it. Perhaps Michael was not aware, but his hands were shaking, and Sam was hyperventilating.

Two shots rang out in quick succession. The first one penetrated Brandon's skull while the second one penetrated Olivia's. For a moment, the entire city seemed to go silent. The connection of the live feed was terminated, and the news presenter was back on screen but she, like everyone else, was at a loss for words. They had witnessed an execution, something that they could not forget until the day they died.

Jefferson's phone vibrated. It was a rather long message

Hello agent, I'm sorry to say that our game of cat and mouse must come to an end. What you saw was a demonstration of my capabilities so I hope you will be wise enough never to stand in my way again. Soon, I will sell off the diamonds and all of it will be over, then you can rest and think about the only failure of your career.

Yours Truly,

Oliver

Jefferson was in shock. *Oliver*. So that was the name of the man who had rained hell on their lives. The man who was responsible for everything. Jefferson Smashed his phone into the wall of the office. The phone splintered, and as it lay on the floor, Jefferson stared at it.

CHAPTER TWENTY-TWO

An abandoned warehouse in NYC:

Oliver was clad in black. He was sitting at a desk and plotting his escape. The details about a certain cruise were displayed on the screen of his laptop. After a long time, he was feeling happy and content. The events so far had gone according to plan, he had robbed the diamonds and the collection, and he had also eliminated the biggest problems. Now all that remained to do was sell the diamonds, conclude the plan with a flourish and then enjoy life.

Oliver felt certain that the FBI agents possessed no threat anymore, they had learned their lesson the hard way. He had also taken the liberty of disclosing his name to the federal agents, and there were two reasons for the same. The first was that he was certain that the feds would not be able to predict his next move, and the second was that Oliver was not his real name.

FBI Field Office, NYC:

Michael and Sam were staring at each other, and Jefferson was sitting in his chair, staring into space. All three of them were well aware of the severity of the crime they had just witnessed. This latest crime had made it even more important for them to catch the thief but none of them could move, they wanted to, but they were unable to. It felt like the shock had slowed down time and dimmed their wits. Their misconception was only broken when the door to Jefferson's office opened again. The agent who had entered had completed only two months with the FBI.

The agent said, "Jefferson, the media is outside the building, they won't go away."

Jefferson did not reply and kept staring at the floor.

Sam said, "Just tell them we do not want to comment right now."

"We did, but they aren't going away, the security has tried to move them back, but we cannot use any force."

Michael said, "Just tell them that we are preparing the official statement."

"I don't think they will go away," said the agent doubtfully.

"Then let them stand!" snapped Michael.

The agent took a hurried leave, but just as he was closing the door, Michal could see that the other agents in the unit were craning their necks from their cubicles to see what was going on in the office.

Sam said, "Jefferson, we need to do something, we can't let him get away with this, with any of this."

Jefferson did not reply.

"Jefferson, all of us are shocked but we need to overcome it," said Michael gently.

Jefferson looked at the two agents in front of him. They didn't realize it, not one of them did. Jefferson was not suffering only from shock. It was the feeling of being defeated, being manipulated and he had never felt that before. He had met criminals before but none of them had made him feel inferior to such an extent. He wondered what mistakes of him were finding his way back to him.

Suddenly Jefferson's office phone rang. He picked it up and waited for the worst to happen, for Oliver's voice to reach his ears, but it didn't. The call was from his wife, the one person who could improve his condition. As Jefferson received the call, Michael and Sam excused themselves from his office; they understood when a man needed space.

Once he had closed the door of the office behind him, Sam said, "So what do you think the guy would do now?"

"His name is Oliver," replied Michael.

"How do you know that?"

"I was standing close to Jefferson, I read the last message he received from the thief."

"And he signed it with his name?" asked Sam disbelievingly

Michael nodded. "He knows that what he did shook us. He thinks we are not a threat anymore."

"Well, he is wrong about that."

"And very soon he is going to realize that."

Evelyn and Rob's Apartment:

Evelyn's hands were shaking, and her head was aching. She had taken two tablets for the pain, but so far, they had done nothing to ease her suffering. She had been at work when she had seen the news. When she had witnessed... the incident, he had dropped the things she had in her hand. Everyone in the store was shocked but Evelyn felt as though she would faint. She had taken a deep breath to steady herself and taken a cab straight home. Rob had been surprised to see her, but he had been concerned, seeing how pale she looked. He had even offered to get her some coffee, knowing very well that he wasn't capable of making a coffee that could be ingested without a grimace.

Now Evelyn was lying down in the bed and Rob was staring at her from the doorway. After a moment of silence, he said, "Sis, did you lose your job?"

"No."

"Then why are you home early?"

"I wasn't feeling very well."

Rob nodded his head maturely. His sister was unwell, which meant she needed to rest. He quietly closed the door behind him as he made his way to the living room. He sat down on the couch to complete his homework but then got an idea. He was concerned for his sister, but this was the perfect opportunity to leave his homework and watch some television. He switched on the television and raised the volume. The news channel was on, but before he could change the channel, his sister literally ran out of the room, took the remote from his hand, and switched off the TV.

"What happened?" asked Rob.

Evelyn just kept the remote down and said, "Nothing. I'm feeling much better now, let's play a game."

"Sure," said Rob

Evelyn heaved a sigh of relief. She could not take the risk of her brother even catching a glimpse of what she had seen.

FBI Field Office, NYC:

Jefferson had just disconnected the call with his wife, and he was feeling much better now. He was still aware of the fact that Oliver had murdered two people, but now, the shock had been replaced by anger.

He looked out of his office to see Michael and Sam discussing something. He knew what they were discussing, and he felt proud. Here were two agents who did not focus on their failures on the attempts made by their opponent to humiliate them, rather they focused on what was important, they focused on how to win so that justice could prevail. His wife had told him something similar. She had told him that he had got this far in life not by focusing on his failures, rather, he had achieved these heights by taking each negative experience as an opportunity to learn and move on.

Moving on. That would be easier said than done in this case. Emotionally speaking, Jefferson had already suppressed the darkness, mentally, he was still shocked, but in terms of leads, he had nothing. The thief had murdered two people right in front of hundreds of thousands of people, but no one had any idea where he was. The only clue they had as of now was the cruise but that was also not very definitive, he could be travelling on any one of the cruises.

Jefferson was feeling as though he was missing something. He felt as though something was right in front of him, but it was still hidden from his view. He opened a file on his computer and went through the details of the various cruises once again. He had finished reading all of them once when he realized something. In fact, he had remembered something which made him realize the truth. The thief had made sure that no one could follow him, he had taken various measures to ensure the same, but the thing which had cost him was his overconfidence.

Jefferson called Michael and Sam into his office. The two agents entered the office and stood at the entrance awkwardly. They didn't know if Jefferson was any better.

Jefferson understood what they were thinking at once. "Michael, close the door and both of you sit down."

The authoritative and calm manner in which Jefferson spoke seemed to assure the two agents that their senior's condition had improved. They gave each other a quick look and then seated themselves on the two vacant chairs in the office.

Jefferson looked at them and said, "I think I know which cruise he will be on."

Michael and Sam looked at each other with astonishment.

"How do you know?" asked Michael.

"Did the thief tell you that too?" asked Sam.

"He might as well have, because the clue he left me leaves little to chance."

"What do you mean?"

"I mean that the thief sent me a message stating that he was going to sell the diamonds soon."

"And how does that tell you which ship he will be on?" asked Michael.

"In the message, he told me that he was going to sell the diamonds soon and that his work here was done."

"So?" prompted Sam, but Michael was quiet, as though he was beginning to see the truth.

"That means he will not stick around long because that will increase the chances of the FBI catching him."

"You mean he will try to leave as early as possible?" asked Sam.

Michael said, "Yes, he is going to leave on the earliest cruise."

"It leaves tomorrow morning, and that gives us about fifteen hours to prepare," stated Jefferson.

"Prepare for what?" asked Michael.

"Prepare to leave, on the same cruise, we are not letting him get away this time."

"But even if we do get on the ship, how will we arrest him?" asked Sam

"That's a good point. We don't know what he looks like, nor do we know the name under which he has purchased the ticket."

"That does pose a challenge, but we know that he is travelling on the ship and what's to say that he isn't doing it for a reason?"

"He just wants to get away, that's his reason."

"But what if it is something more than that? A cruise with a limited number of guests and limited surveillance is the best place to exchange goods, even stolen ones."

Michael's eyes widened. "So, you think he and his buyer will be there and that is where the exchange will take place?"

"Correct, so all we have to do is get on that ship and keep a close eye on as many guests as possible and I have a plan to flush the thief out into the open."

"What's the plan?" asked Sam.

"Let's just say I'll be forcing him to panic and thus reveal his identity to us."

CHAPTER TWENTY-THREE

Jefferson's house:

Later that night, Martha was packing a bag for her husband with a very troubled expression on her face. Until now, her husband had been after a thief, but now he was chasing a dangerous murderer who possessed the guts to kill two people on live television. The fact that she was the wife of an FBI agent and a journalist herself did not mean that she wasn't concerned for her husband's safety. On the contrary, being a reporter meant that she was very well aware of the risk involved in pursuing a dangerous lead. Nearly every week, she heard about a source, a reporter or a lawman who had been injured due to a story or case they were working on. Her mind was constantly thinking about ways to talk her husband out of going on the cruise when the man himself entered the room.

Jefferson looked at his wife and said, 'What's the matter, Martha? You look very tense."

"That is because I am," replied his wife shortly, while packing her husband's bag at the same time.

"And may I know why?"

"Do I have to tell you? The man you are following has proved today that he is neither afraid nor hesitant to commit a murder."

Jefferson sat down beside his wife and placing a hand on her knee, he said, "Martha you know the risks involved in my job better than anyone."

"I know, but this time it is different, it's personal, and the man is trying his best to…" Martha faltered.

Her husband looked at her with concerned eyes. He knew that what he was doing involved considerable risk, and that would make convincing his wife even more difficult. As it is, he was under pressure from the bureau. Oliver had committed an act of terrorism, and such acts were not tolerable. If he had not argued strongly against the matter, the case would have been in the hands of the anti-terrorism unit by now. But Jefferson had assured his superiors that the problem would be resolved at the earliest possible and based on his stellar record, they had agreed to let him continue to work on the case.

Jefferson looked at his wife and said, "Look, Martha, it is my job to put thieves behind bars, and I know how to take care of myself. Besides, as you said, he is the one who has made it personal."

"It is not wise to knowingly venture into dangerous territory while unaware of the plans of your opponent," said Martha.

Jefferson smiled and said, "While I agree that quote would look quite attractive on a T-shirt, I must inform you that I am aware of the plans of my opponent."

"And how is that?"

Jefferson explained his theory to his wife. He told her how and why he suspected that Oliver would be commuting on the cruise. The worry lines never left Martha's forehead, but her eyes conveyed the message that her brain was constantly computing the information and keeping up with what her husband was telling her.

"So, this is your best chance," she concluded.

"Our best and possibly the last chance to catch him, we cannot make any mistakes."

Michael's apartment:

Michael was done with his arrangements for leaving. His bags were packed with a lot of time to spare but Michael was one of the people who hated rushing things, he preferred to plan everything and then complete the task with precision. He was sitting in a chair with a can of soda in his hand, and his eyes were trained on the schematics of the cruise ship, which were displayed on his laptop screen. He had borrowed these schematics from Sam with the intention of studying the battlefield before the action began.

The vessel that the three agents were scheduled to board was equipped with all the modern equipment for traveling and navigating along with the best services and amenities for the guests. The security was top-notch, but to ensure the privacy of the guests, the number of cameras and surveillance devices had been kept as low as possible. While the cameras would be covering all the areas of common access, but due to their sparse number, there were some angles and certain specific places which would be left out. Michael had groaned when he realized this, and the reason was obvious. Fewer cameras meant more blind spots and more blind spots meant more places where they would have to personally keep an eye.

The three of them were boarding the craft under aliases. While the captain and certain key crew members would be aware of their true identities, the larger part of the passengers and crew would think of them as ordinary citizens on a pleasure trip. Their cover story was simple. They were three friends who had been awarded the cruise from their company as a reward for their hard work. It was an all-expenses paid trip, one on which the three of them were supposed to enjoy themselves. But the truth was that not even one of the agents had the thought of relaxing in their minds. Every one of them had their reasons for being passionate about the mission, and Michael's was his future. He was aware that this was his last chance, his last chance to prove himself, to achieve what he wanted, to live the life that he wanted.

He had clearly displayed his dislike for the thieves but what he had seen on the television, the murder, was enough to appeal to his sense of justice and his heart full of compassion. Brandon and Olivia were thieves, but they did not deserve to die. That was something wrong, and Michael had every intention of righting the wrongs that had been committed.

There was no way that the thief would not recognize them the moment they stepped on that ship, but he would not dare to do anything as that would risk exposing his identity, and that included trying to get away. This was the final act, their last chance, everything had to be factored in and nothing could go wrong.

Michael remembered his childhood, how he had always wanted to work for the FBI, he remembered how he had gotten to know about the successes of Jefferson Brown. The first time he had made up his mind to join the FBI was when he had learned about the cases which had been brought to a successful conclusion by Jefferson Brown. He was just thirteen years old then, but he had his work cut out for him. He had studied hard and trained, and the extent of his motivation was such that he had ended up being one of the youngest FBI special agents. His dream of working with Jefferson had come true and now was his test. This would be the very first time that they would be in close proximity of their adversary, they would not know who he was, but he would know, and he would keep a close eye on them.

Suddenly, Michael heard his doorbell ring, assuming it to be the pizza which he had ordered, Michael walked briskly up to the door and opened it to realize his deduction was right. After he had taken and placed the pizza box on the table, he got another can of soda from the fridge, opened it and then, while taking a swig from the can in his hand, he opened the box of pizza, after which he promptly choked on the soda. The reason for Michael's reaction was that sitting in the middle of the pizza, among the tomatoes and cheese, there was a single chit of paper with four words printed across it – *How are you, Michael?*

A hotel in NYC:

Oliver was packing his bags with enthusiasm. The entirety of Oliver's luggage comprised of just two bags, one for his clothes and the other one for his electronic appliances. Everyone needed a good holiday, even thieves, but when that holiday also showed prospects of being largely rewarding, the wait was unbearable. After he was satisfied that he had packed everything that he needed, Oliver stashed his bags in the corner of the room and set to work. When you are a thief, certain things become a reflex. Checking and noting the exits of any place one visited, not attracting any unwanted attention, trying to blend in with the crowd, not giving your real name to anyone and of course, securing your wallets and other possessions to make sure that the other people who were in the same profession did not end up making you their target. All of this was natural, but the most important thing, which is the first lesson that a thief learns and the first habit which they acquire, is not to leave tracks.

Oliver opened a bottle of alcohol, took some of it on a cotton pad and began his exercise. He wiped each and every surface of the room, as anything he had touched could prove to be his mistake and a clue for the cops. After thoroughly wiping the room, he felt tired and sweaty. It was hard work, especially when you had to do it all without the aid of any machine. Oliver wiped his forehead, immediately, he looked at his hand and his eyes widened, he ran to the washroom and locked the door behind him.

Sam's Apartment:

Sam had just come back from the departmental store. He had packed his bags, but he was missing one very important thing – extra batteries. Whenever Sam went on a trip, he made sure to not only pack a torch but also pack some extra batteries. It was something that he had done since he was a child. Although there had been only a few times when he had actually used the torch, it was good knowing that it was in his possession. One could not always rely only on the flashlight of their smartphone.

Sam's mind was constantly thinking about what would happen in the next few days of his life, there were infinite possibilities of the events which might occur but what he hoped for was the best version, the too-good-to-be-true version. After he was done with his packing, his mind wandered to the one thing which he did not want to think about – Olivia and Brandon. While they were alive, Sam always saw them as offenders of the law, nothing more, but now he felt as though he had lost friends. Without realizing it, he had begun to see Olivia and Brandon as friends and the feelings he had for them were those that one had for teammates. In his mind, Sam was sure of one thing, he would do whatever it took to get Oliver.

CHAPTER TWENTY-FOUR

Jefferson was waiting for Michael and Sam to arrive in his office. It was early morning and for the first time in his life, Jefferson was in his office in informal attire. He was dressed in jeans and a T-shirt with his sunglasses hanging from the front of his T-shirt. Usually, people are comparatively uncomfortable while dressed formally, but that was not true in Jefferson's case. The man was more comfortable in a suit than an ordinary person would be in their pyjamas. Jefferson checked the time on his watch and frowned, the other two were late. He was the one who had the necessary documents for their respective aliases, but they were useless if they did not reach the ship before cast-off. Just as he took out his phone and dialed Sam's number, he heard a ringtone just outside his office door.

Sam and Michael entered the office and, declining the call, Sam smirked.

"The number you are calling is currently busy, please try later."

"Any later and we would have missed it," grumbled Jefferson as he handed the two agents white envelopes.

After securing their credentials, the three agents headed to the building exit. Instead of taking one of the cars of the bureau, they took a cab, for obvious reasons, and proceeded to the docks. They reached and boarded the ship with some time to spare and after meeting with the captain they were escorted to their respective cabins. The cabins were not what you would expect on a cruise, in a positive way. They had every commodity provided in a luxury hotel room, including large portholes to admire the view. The cabins were spacious and comfortable, but the three agents didn't have time to admire their surroundings. They unanimously decided that the very first thing that they should do upon boarding was to tour the vessel and thus, all three of them just dumped their bags in their respective cabins and began their inspection.

The ship consisted of three levels and comprised of a pool, a bar, a lounge, and a dining hall. The lounge was quite spacious and was divided into three parts. One of the parts served as a small but rather well-equipped library with titles in multiple languages, the middle area was furnished with leather couches and armchairs, serving as a sort of common sitting area whereas a specific area of the lounge had also been set up as the game zone and thus, there were a few casino gaming machines located there.

The guests had access to all the areas of the ship except the kitchen, engine room, captain's cabin, the bridge and the crew area. Out of the total six decks of the ship, the majority of the cabins were located on the second and third decks while a few were situated on the fourth deck. It was Michael's understanding that the ones located on the second and third deck were standard cabins, but the few cabins located on the fourth deck were even more luxurious. The number of passengers on the ship was considerably less than what the agents had previously expected, which was quite an advantage. There were large windows and portholes in each and every location on the ship which looked out on the beautiful view outside. In all, if the agents did not have work to do, then they would have really enjoyed themselves.

After inspecting every nook and corner of the ship thoroughly, the three joined the other passengers on the primary deck as the ship cast off and the shore grew distant with each passing moment. Once the shore was out of sight, the three agents turned their attention to the other passengers in turn. The bunch of people around them were varied but the two things which they had in common were their ample bank balances and the smiles on their faces. Each one of them was in possession of secrets, so were the three agents, and so was every other human on the face of the earth, but the agents were after the secrets of a single person.

As the ship gained speed, the people began drifting off to their cabins or to the bar. The ones with weak abdomens headed to their room to rest, while the ones who did not mind the motion of the ship, or enjoyed it, were the ones who decided to start their holiday with a drink. The three agents took this as an opportunity to get to know some of the guests and thus, they also followed the latter group. There was a very worried expression on Michael's face as he walked towards the bar, the expression that one has when one is confronting their worst enemy.

(II)

Oliver was sitting in his cabin and his face was contorted into an expression of fury. He had believed that the agents would have learned their lesson, but here they were, on the very same ship on which Oliver was travelling, with the diamonds. This was no coincidence, even a fool could make that out, but the question was how they had figured out where he would be. He had been very careful not to leave a trail, and he had even inquired about various cruises departing on different dates to cover his tracks and yet, the three meddlers had shown up as his co-passengers. Although Oliver had been smart enough not to carry the items which he had stolen from the younger Williamson's collection, but he had no choice but to bring the diamonds with him. The items from the collection had been sent ahead by him to a safe location from where he could retrieve them whenever he wanted, and now he wished that the diamonds were also with those items, safe.

Oliver got up from the chair and walked to the porthole. His cabin was located on the fourth deck and the view was magnificent, a view he had planned to enjoy, and he would have, had his plans not been disrupted by the same trio again. Even though the arrival of the three agents was unwanted and unexpected, Oliver was the sort of person who hoped for things to go as expected but had plans just in case they didn't and very often, these plans were the ones which got him out of tough situations, much like the one which he currently found himself in. He had the diamonds with him, but they were hidden, so well hidden that even if his antagonists were staring right at them, they would not realize it. But that was not the hard part, the hard part was interacting with the agents and not giving himself away, being in the vicinity and not showing the slightest signs of nervousness. He didn't just have to act that he was innocent, he had to believe that he was innocent, and that was very difficult, considering what he had done and what he intended to do.

(III)

Michael was sitting in the lounge with a glass of lemonade in his hand. He had tried his best to divert his attention from the alcohol in the bar, but it was like trying to focus on the moon during the day, it just wasn't possible. That was why he had just taken his glass of lemonade and had come to the lounge. The people who were in his close vicinity included a woman of around fifty years of age, a rather dangerous-looking young man, a half-asleep man, and a young woman with her head bent down into the book. He knew that the middle-aged woman would probably be the easiest and the best person to talk to, but he felt certain that Oliver would not be the name of a fifty year old woman and thus, he decided to start a conversation with the man who had the pleasant looks of a goon.

Michael said, "That's a splendid book that you are reading."

The man, who had been reading "Twenty Thousand Leagues Under The Sea" by Jules Verne, said, "Indeed, have you read it?"

"I did, although I must say it was quite a long time back, so I'm a little fuzzy on the details."

"Surely you can't forget Captain Nemo."

"Of course not! Nor can I forget Monsieur Arronox, Conseil, Ned land and of course, the Nautilus."

The man gave a lopsided smile and said, "I thought you said you were a little fuzzy about the details."

"Well, I can't tell you the scientific names of the species they encountered, they were a *little* complicated."

Both men laughed. The man outstretched his hand and said, "Will Singer."

"John Beck," said Michael giving the hand a slight shake.

"So, John, you are a businessman?"

"I wish! But I work for an MNC, worked hard, and got this holiday as a reward."

"Good for you! What do you do?"

"I work in the accounts department, what about you?"

"Shipping business, being on a cruise, quite ironic don't you think?"

"It is, indeed. What's the name of your company?"

Will raised an eyebrow and said, "Poseidon Shipping, why? Got something you want to get across the waters?"

Michael looked up sharply, there was something odd about the man's tone. "What?"

"Nothing," said Will getting up "It was nice meeting you."

"The pleasure was all mine," replied Michael, as Will got up and departed.

The way Will had offered Michael to get something "across the water" made Michael feel as though he was talking to an offender of the law. The man had quite a good chance of being the person who was buying the diamonds from Oliver, and Michael made up his mind to keep an eye on him. Michael looked up and to his surprise, he saw the middle-aged woman staring at him. He gave a slight smile and went away, looking back once he was at the exit, only to confront the brown eyes of the woman seated in the armchair once again.

As Michael was heading to his cabin, he saw Sam approaching him from the opposite direction.

"Found anything yet?" asked Sam.

"Nothing of immediate value, what about you? And Jefferson?"

"Well, I tried talking to some people but they genuinely looked as though they were just to enjoy the cruise, not sell or buy diamonds and as far as Jefferson is concerned, the man is a chameleon, no one can tell what his real intentions are just by looking at him, there he is, laughing away."

Following the direction in which Sam's finger pointed, Michael saw Jefferson chatting with a couple and laughing but just as the pair departed, Jefferson's expression turned serious, and he walked towards the place where Sam and

Michael were standing.

"When do you plan to put your plan into action?" asked Sam.

"And more importantly, what is your plan?" added Michael.

Jefferson looked around and said, "Not here and not until the day after tomorrow, we need to give everyone some time to settle before we try anything."

Michael nodded and once again, they headed their separate ways.

Till dinnertime that evening, the federal agents spent their time interacting with the other passengers but could not get any clue which might assist them. The only positive thing which had occurred was that Michael had found an acquaintance. Just a few hours before the time for the evening meal, Michael was on the deck when he happened to strike up a conversation with another passenger, a bachelor, named Gary with a zeal for playing chess. Such was the passion of the man towards the game, that he had even convinced Michael to face off with him in a match on the expensive-looking chess board. After crossing their tactical swords for a duration of fifty minutes, the game was drawn with the consent of both the players.

"This was splendid, John!" said Gary.

"Yes, it was!"

"We should certainly play again."

"We definitely will," said Michael and headed to his cabin and as he looked back, he saw that Gary had reset the board and was busy playing against himself.

(IV)

It was late evening and Jefferson was sitting in his cabin. He had tried to search for clues the entire day but to no avail, however, his mood had been uplifted by the splendid meal which he had just done justice to. Now, with his stomach full and his mind clear, he began thinking about what they would do next. He planned to devote the next twenty-four hours to further scrutinize the guests and also set his plan into motion. The plan which he had in mind was not complex, however, there was little doubt about the chances of its success.

Thinking of the plan had reminded Jefferson to check on something, he got up and went to the *armoire* located in the cabin. Opening it, he took out a small box and one look at its contents was enough to reassure Jefferson that his plan was quite decent.

CHAPTER TWENTY-FIVE

Another day passed by without the agents making any breakthrough. Although, unknown to Michael and Sam, Jefferson had met with the captain of the ship and entrusted him with the contents of the box. The contents, apart from being a crucial part of Jefferson's plan were also a sign of the years Jefferson had spent in law enforcement and the connections he had on the legal side as well as in the gray area.

On the third day of the cruise, Jefferson awoke early in the morning, got dressed and waited for the knock on his door. The previous night, He had instructed Michael and Sam to come to his room first thing in the morning and accordingly, they were at his door at six. After the three of them were seated, Jefferson finally let them in on his plan. He explained every step in detail, along with the significance of the object in the box. After he was done, the two agents gave each other a silent look.

"Will he fall for that?" asked Sam.

"Even if he doesn't, he will not be able to resist the urge to check on the diamonds and his facial expressions and body language will be more than sufficient to reveal his identity to us."

"But how do you plan to watch all the people at once?"

"Simple. We assemble them in the lounge because it is big enough and has cameras. I'll be monitoring the footage myself."

"You mean *we* will be monitoring the footage," said Michael.

"No, I mean *I*, you two will be in the lounge."

"That's just great!" retorted Sam.

Michael got up and said, "Then let's get to work, what's our reason for assembling the guests?"

"We keep it simple, just tell them that the captain has an important announcement to make."

Michael left with the intention of going to the captain's cabin.

Sam looked at Jefferson and said, "What do we do once we know who he is? How do we confront him and get the diamonds?"

"We'll cross that bridge when we get to it," said Jefferson before exiting the room.

After a rather hurried breakfast, Jefferson headed to the surveillance room, while Michael and Sam went to the lounge. They took seats on opposite sides of the room and waited for the announcement. After a wait of just two minutes, a voice reached their ears. The voice belonged to the captain, and it was booming through the electronic announcer which was fitted in every location on the ship. The announcement was short and precise, the passengers of the cruise were requested to assemble in the lounge as the captain had an important announcement to make. Michael and Sam saw as, within minutes, all the passengers on the ship were assembled. Once more, Michael was grateful for the fact that the number of passengers on board was low.

After a minute had passed, the captain entered the lounge with a grave expression, in his hand he had a small box, the same box which Jefferson had given him.

"Ladies and gentlemen, as all of you are aware, I have an important announcement to make, and I prefer to make it face-to-face."

A murmur of agreement passed around the room. Michael and Sam were looking at each passenger very closely. Although Michael tried to focus his attention equally on each passenger, he found that he could not help but focus a bit more on Will Singer. The man in question seemed to be ill at ease as he smoked a cigarette, taking a long drag each time.

"I will not beat around the bush. As you will be aware, the famous collection of diamonds, *Les Morceaux de Lumiere* has been stolen recently, now, we have a situation on board." saying this the captain opened the box and took out its contents. Everyone gasped as they saw what rested in the palm of the captain's hand. There, lying in the center of the palm, lay a glittering diamond.

The captain ran a quick eye through the crowd and so did Michael and Sam. In the surveillance room, Jefferson was not even blinking, his eyes were glued to the screen, and he was trying to look for any signs of nervousness. But that was quite a job, as everyone had a look of surprise on their faces. He could see Michael and Sam, who were now on their feet, looking at each passenger in turn.

Back in the lounge, the captain said, "This is one of those diamonds. Now, I strongly urge all of you to share any information you might have regarding the diamond or about the identity of the person who has smuggled it on board."

The captain looked expectantly at the faces of each of the passengers but none of them said anything. They just looked at each other's faces with either suspicious or confused eyes.

After a few moments of expectant silence, the captain spoke up once again, "If any one of you wishes to talk to me privately, they can come to my office. I look forward to your cooperation."

After the captain had left the lounge, there was an awkward environment in the lounge. Each passenger looked at the other with apprehensive eyes. Soon the numbers began decreasing as the people exited the lounge to clear their heads. Michael looked up at the camera as a signal to Jefferson that it was up to him now. Once again, the only inhabitants of the lounge were Sam and Michael.

Sam walked over to where Michael was sitting. "Did you notice anything? Anyone who might have reacted strangely or who looked too surprised?"

"Nope, but I did see someone who was *not* surprised. We need to keep an eye on Will Singer."

Sam looked at Michael and said, "The tall chap? Why?"

"Like I said, he wasn't surprised, and that would make sense if he already knew that the diamonds were on board."

"So, you think that he realized that the diamond which the captain had was a fake?"

"Could be. Anyhow, let's check on Jefferson."

Within minutes, Sam and Michael were standing in the surveillance room talking to Jefferson.

"What did you see? Anything out of the ordinary?" asked Jefferson.

"Nothing other than general surprise on my end," said Sam.

"Same with me, except in the case of Will Singer," said Michael.

Jefferson raised an eyebrow and said, "What do you mean?"

Michael told him what he had seen and what his theory was, and Jefferson nodded along. After listening intently to what Michael told him, Jefferson said, "That is an interesting theory, more so because Will was one of the four passengers who went straight to their rooms after the announcement was made."

"Who're the other three?" asked Michael and Sam in unison.

Jefferson beckoned them towards the monitor, on which four screenshots were displayed. Each one had the face of a passenger opening their room, with the timestamp on one corner of the monitor. Michael recognized the middle-aged woman he had met in the lounge, Will Singer, another man named Francis and a woman named Dorothy.

"And we suspect these four because we presume that the thief would have the diamonds in their room, correct?" asked Sam.

"That is the most secure place, and the thief can check the diamonds whenever he wants. Keeping the diamonds on his person is risky and so is hiding them somewhere on the ship where any crew member could easily find them," replied Jefferson.

"And why do we even suspect the women? Surely, they couldn't be our thief," said Sam.

"Sam, we know that the thief is cunning. While it may be true that the odds indicate that he is male, but remember, don't ignore Dorothy and the middle-aged woman because we think our thief is male, he could have always lied to us about his name."

"But we saw him on the..." began Sam.

"There is no guarantee that the person we saw was the thief, it could be anyone!"

Michael said, "So as of now, these four are our primary suspects, correct?"

"Precisely, we need to keep an eye on them at all times."

"I'll take Will, my gut says he is up to no good," said Michael and went out.

"I'll tail Dorothy, there is no law against following a beautiful suspect, is there?" joked Sam and headed out.

Both the agents had left, thinking that they had cleverly left Jefferson with not one but two suspects to surveil, but Jefferson knew that very well, he just didn't think it was important. He didn't mind working hard, because that was the only assured way to obtain the desired results.

(II)

Michael was on the deck and was pretending to read a book while his eyes were fixed on Will, who was talking to another passenger. They seemed to be having a funny conversation as the two men kept bursting into laughter from time to time. Various thoughts were going through Michael's mind. He was trying to formulate a plan to get the thief to tell them where he had hidden the diamonds, but he saw no way of doing that without alerting Oliver in the process. To prepare a plan which would guarantee results they had to identify their thief first but as of now, it could be any one of the four suspects.

Suddenly Michael heard a voice calling the name "John", at first, he did not react but then, with a start, he realized that everyone knew *him* as John and that the person was addressing him. He turned to find Gary standing a little distance away, with his chess set tucked under his arm.

He came towards Michael and said, "Want to have a game of chess? You won't always manage to draw the game with me."

Michael's first instinct was to refuse the offer, but then he saw that Will was heading towards the lounge and realized that he would be able to keep an eye on him under the pretence of playing chess with Gary.

"Sure, let's go to the lounge."

Michael and Gary headed to the lounge and just before they entered, Michael saw that along with Will, the old woman was also seated there. The situation Michael found himself in was the perfect one for achieving two objectives at the same time.

(III)

Dorothy was in the dining hall, enjoying a cup of coffee. One of the people in her current surroundings was another passenger named Logan Young. For some reason, the man kept shooting periodic glances in her direction and that annoyed her to such an extent that she decided to confront the man.

"May I help you?"

The man looked surprised. "Excuse me?"

"You keep looking at me, is there something you would like to say?"

Sam did the only thing which could have saved him - he complimented the woman. "I'm sorry, but I just couldn't help myself, your eyes are stunning."

Unfortunately for Sam, that did not work. Dorothy said, "Did you think you could get away by complimenting me?"

"I must admit that I did, but I presume I've failed that endeavor?"

"Quite so, so tell me the real reason."

"Believe it or not, that was the real reason, but if it makes you uncomfortable, I'll leave."

"I think it would be better if you did," replied the woman in a cold manner.

Sam departed rather hurriedly and once he was outside, he shook his head. He was fool to look at her in a way that she felt uncomfortable, he was just doing his job, surveillance, but he would not be able to do it any longer if he kept getting himself in situations like these.

Sam took a quick look inside to see that the woman had settled comfortably in her chair once again. He leaned against the wall in the hallway and looked out towards the deck at the other end of the hallway, trying to think of a way around the latest obstacle, when he saw Jefferson come into his field of vision. Sam walked briskly towards the deck and weaving around a couple of passengers he caught up with Jefferson.

"Hey!"

Jefferson turned and said, "Hey Logan..." and in a whispered tone, he added, "What're you doing?"

"I think you should go for a coffee in the dining hall," said Sam with a wide smile.

"What? But I need to go to the..."

"I'll go to the little video place. Why don't you just head over for some coffee? You look like you could use some caffeine."

Jefferson understood and nodded. After he was gone, Sam heaved a sigh of relief, that solved the problem. Smiling to himself and avoiding the gaze of his fellow passengers, he went up to the "little video place" which was also known as the surveillance room.

(IV)

Later that night, the three agents convened in Michael's room for a short meeting. They had worked on their respective assignment for the entire day and now was the time to discuss the conclusions they had formed.

"So, what have we got?" asked Jefferson.

"Nothing, absolutely nothing, your plan gave us suspects but we have nothing to identify the real thief from the lot," complained Michael.

"We cannot keep going on like this, just watching the suspects the entire day did not yield any results," stated Sam.

"I'm open to suggestions," said Jefferson shortly and looked at the other two meaningfully, but they fell silent. Jefferson did not blame them, it was a difficult situation, one that had to be managed delicately and yet with speed. In such situations, it was the easiest thing to lose your cool and make a mistake, but it was Jefferson's job to see that they did not do so.

"We still have time, the cruise will continue for a few more days and that means that the thief will be on board, and we will be able to catch him. Rest, don't overexert yourself, we'll meet tomorrow morning to discuss what we should do next."

Sam and Michael departed soon after. Michael went to his room and shut the door, he then closed his eyes and attempted to go to sleep. He spent the first few minutes just lying on the bed with his eyes open, but after a while, sleep found him. But suddenly, he heard a gunshot and woke up to realize that he was bleeding.

CHAPTER TWENTY-SIX

Michael woke up with a start. There were beads of cold sweat on his forehead and the room was pitch dark. His heart was banging against his ribs and the darkness of his cabin seemed to close around him. It was a dream, but it felt so real. Nightmares usually did. He could hear the sound of rain and the waves crashing against each other along with the slight sway of the ship which indicated that the weather conditions were not favorable.

Michael got up from the bed and took a sip of water from the glass on his bedside table. He couldn't sleep now, not after what he had just dreamt. In times like these, one could lie down and waste their time, or they could get some work done. Choosing the latter alternative, Michael exited his cabin to go to the surveillance room of the ship. As he walked through the corridor, he could feel the freezing wind strike his skin and make his hair stand on an end. He wished to get a jacket from his room, but now he had come too far to go back. He took the stairs, two at a time, walked at a brisk pace and found himself knocking on the closed door of the surveillance room within five minutes. The door was opened by a guard who looked the worse for sleep, and he gave Michael a look which clearly expressed the extent of his annoyance. Luckily, he was one of the crew members who knew the true identity of Michael, so he stepped aside at once to let him enter the room. Once inside, Michael closed the door behind him and felt much better than before. There was a watch on a side table, probably the guard's, and its hands pointed at half past one. Michael hadn't realized that it was so late, nevertheless, he had work to do.

He sat down at the computer and decided to inspect the footage of the time when the captain had made the announcement earlier in the day. He went through each frame of the video feed from the different cameras, but he could not find anything. His mind was on the verge of giving up when he noticed something. It was nothing much, but it was odd, and that led to Michael pausing the video and zooming in, and that was when he saw it. Their biggest clue, the breakthrough they had been looking for, was staring right at him, along with a face, a face that was familiar to Michael. Michael wanted to call Jefferson right away but then he stopped, a thought had just crossed his mind. What if he chased the lead on his own? What if he closed the case and proved to Jefferson that he was good enough? These thoughts forced Michael's hand to replace his mobile back in his pocket. He quickly scanned through the live feed from the cameras to determine the current location of his suspect, and within a minute, he had the information he wanted. This was an opportunity and Michael had no intention of wasting it. He sprang up from his chair and departed from the surveillance room in a hurry. His manner was quick and sure, and his mind was focused.

Michael entered the bar with a brisk gait and saw a man sitting on one of the high stools. The bartender was serving the man another drink and after he was done, Michael sat down on the stool beside the man, who looked at Michael and gave a look of surprise.

"Still up?"

"Yes, can't seem to sleep, what about you Gary?"

"Same with me, it's this rain, it makes me nervous."

"The rain makes you nervous? I should have thought it was something else."

"Something else? What do you mean?"

"Nothing. So, what do you think about what the captain said, got any information?"

"Yeah, I wish! There is no thief who would let himself get caught by leaving a trail."

"Even the most skilled thieves make mistakes, I'm speaking from experience."

The bartender had been listening to their conversation with great interest, now he looked at Michael and said, "Can I get you anything, sir?"

Michael eyed the various bottles of alcohol on display. "Just lemonade, thanks."

Michael looked at the stool on the other side of Gary and said, "Still carrying around your chess set?"

"Yep, I love it."

"You sure it's the game you love?"

"You know what Michael, if I didn't know better, I'd say you were drunk."

Michael laughed as he sipped the lemonade which the bartender had placed in front of him. He said, "Want to play a game?"

Gary's eyes lit up. "Sure! I'll just set the board."

"Somewhere in private, not here."

"The lounge?"

"How about my room?"

"Let's have a game in mine," suggested Gary. "It's closer."

Michael agreed. Gary was looking for something in his pocket, after a moment he got out his room key and then promptly dropped it on the floor. Michael immediately bent down to pick it up and handed it back to its owner.

"Thanks a lot, I guess I drank a little more than I'm used to. Anyway, let's just finish our drinks and then start the game as soon as possible."

Michael gave Gary a thumbs-up as he sipped his lemonade. There was something odd, but he couldn't understand what. Perhaps it was just the excitement. Michael had drained his glass within minutes and so had Gary. They got up and went to Gary's room. The timing was highly inconvenient, but now, Michael was feeling sleepy. He shook his head a few times and tried to focus on what he planned to do.

Gary opened the door to his room, and they entered. While Gary was setting up the board, Michael was scrutinizing his movements. He was showing no signs of distress or nervousness.

After the board was set up, Before Michael could make the first move, Gary stopped him.

"Wait a minute, let's make this more interesting."

He got up and opened the cupboard in his room. From there he got out a small bottle of alcohol and picked up the glasses from the side table. He poured two drinks and offered one of the glasses to Michael.

"No thanks," said Michael shortly and pushed the glass away.

"Oh, come on! Take it, it opens your mind!"

Michael ignored him and made the first move.

Gary looked at him and said, "Either you drink, or the game is off."

Michael looked at him and said, "Just play the game, I don't want to drink."

"Are you a kid? You're not prohibited to take a sip you know."

"I don't want to," said Michael sternly.

"Ok! Your wish."

Gary sat down and they played in silence for a few minutes. Michael kept making mistakes and losing his pieces. For some reason, he couldn't concentrate, his eyelids felt heavy and his mind dull. The rain was falling with much more intensity now, and Michael could feel his head throbbing. After a moment he realized that Gary was waiting for him to make his move. He was about to move his bishop when Gary spoke up.

"Do you know my real name?"

Michael looked up sharply and said, "What?"

"It's Oliver, the thief you're after."

Michael blinked a few times and tried to get up, but he couldn't.

"Don't bother, I slipped a drug into your lemonade. All you can do is listen, so listen carefully."

Michael said, "I know."

"Know what?"

"Where the diamonds are..."

"And how do you know that?"

Michael shook his head a few times before replying. He said, "Saw you in the footage...checking...chess."

"Let me fill in the blanks for you," said Oliver "So you saw me in the camera footage, checking the chess pieces after the captain made the announcement? Smart. I figured you idiots would look for the ones who went to their rooms or someplace else, not the lounge. Anyway, that's right, I did check the chess pieces after the captain's announcement, I must say, you got me good."

Saying this, Oliver picked up the kings, the queens, and a knight. He then overturned the pieces and from their large bases, he took out five diamonds – *Les Morceau De Lumiere.* Michael's eyes widened and he tried to snatch the diamonds from Oliver's grasp, but Oliver punched him across the jaw, and he fell down to the floor.

"Well, Michael, I must say this was fun, but like all things, this must come to an end. Rest assured, you have ruined my deal, but there are always more buyers."

"Who was your buyer?" groaned Michael

"Oh, nice try, but both of us know, I won't tell you that."

Oliver got a small bag from his *armoire* and opening it, he extracted a small radio. He tuned into the right frequency and said, "It's me, bring it around."

After replacing the radio back into the bag, he looked at Michael who had stood up by taking the support of the bed.

"That was my emergency transportation, it's on the way, which means it is time for us to part."

Oliver moved towards Michael menacingly. Michael tried to defend, but the drug had dimmed his senses, he received heavy blows from Oliver and was soon knocked out on the floor once again. Oliver picked up the bottle of alcohol from the side table and sprinkled the contents onto Michael's face and shirt. Then, he exited the cabin and went to the deck. Rain was falling quite heavily but Oliver saw a small boat at some distance. He signaled the captain with a flashlight and when the boat was in range, Oliver secured his bag and dove into the cold water.

CHAPTER TWENTY-SEVEN

The sound of the ship's emergency alarm woke up Jefferson. He looked at the watch and then, grabbing his jacket, he hurried out of the room. He could hear people shouting and running footsteps. The passengers were coming out of their rooms, confused and disoriented. Jefferson saw Sam coming towards his room, weaving through the passengers and crew of the ship.

"What happened?" asked Jefferson in a loud voice.

"Don't know yet!" replied Sam "Apparently someone had gone overboard and one of the guards saw it in the camera."

"Who is it?"

"Don't know, let's find out."

Jefferson and Sam ran towards the surveillance room. On their way, they could see a crew member running a large searchlight over the waves and another one trying to pierce the veil of darkness by using binoculars.

Jefferson opened the door to the surveillance room, to find the captain and the first mate inside.

"Captain, what happened?"

"A passenger just jumped overboard!" exclaimed the captain.

"Jumped? Willingly?" asked Sam incredulously.

"Yes! He had a bag with him, here, see for yourself," saying this the captain turned one of the monitors in the room towards the two agents. All eyes were focused on the screen as the video was played, they could clearly see one man, who was careful not to show his face in the camera, signal someone using a flashlight and then, after a moment, jump overboard without the slightest hesitation.

The captain paused the video and said, "The guard saw the man and that was why he raised the alarm, it's a standard protocol."

"Do we know who it was?" asked Jefferson.

"Not yet, we plan to check each and every passenger and crew worker with the list just to make sure."

Suddenly Sam said, "Where's Michael? He would have heard the alarm too."

The guard who had been standing in the corner to let his superiors handle the situation said, "Michael? You mean the other fed?"

"Yes," said Jefferson. "You know where he is?"

"Yeah, he came over some time ago to look at some footage and then left in a hurry."

Sam and Jefferson exchanged a quick look. "What footage did he see?"

A few minutes later, Sam and Jefferson were running towards Gary's cabin. They had seen the footage and now they knew where Michael went. They knew that he had gone to the bar and then he had come out with Gary a few minutes later, only to go with him in his cabin.

Sam took a position on the side of the door, with his gun in his hand while Jefferson banged open the door. Each of the two agents entered the room in defensive positions with their guns at shoulder level, ready for defense or offense. But they saw no danger. The only thing they saw was Michael's crumpled figure on the floor.

"My god!" exclaimed Sam, as he rushed forward to check Michael's vitals.

Jefferson banged open the door of the washroom to check if someone was concealed there, however, he realized that they were the only inhabitants of the cabin. He looked at Sam and was surprised to see the look he had on his face. It was a look of absolute disgust.

"What's the matter Sam? Is he all right?"

"Oh yes, just had a little too much to drink."

"What do you mean?"

"Come here and see for yourself."

Just as Jefferson came close to where Michael was lying, the sweet scent of alcohol reached his nostrils. He looked at Sam and then at Michael, the situation was clear as day. Michael had broken his oath, he had drunk alcohol and under its influence, he had warned the thief that they were onto him and thus, the thief had made his dramatic escape.

Jefferson could not control himself, he slapped Michael across his face. Michael's eyes fluttered open and focused on the faces of the two people in front of him.

"Jefferson? Sam?" then his eyes widened. "Oliver, he was on the ship, it was Gary!"

Sam helped him up roughly and made him sit on the bed.

"Don't worry, we can handle the job from here, *our job*."

Michael looked at Sam with a questioning look on his face, but Sam just looked at him and shook his head. Michael looked at Jefferson who was looking at him with an infuriated expression.

"What happened, why are you looking at me like that?"

"Did you even hesitate before you did it?" asked Jefferson.

"Did what?"

"Broke your promise and betrayed us!" exclaimed Sam.

"What are you talking about? I didn't betray anyone!"

"You know, Michael, it takes guts to lie when you are walking proof of your betrayal."

"Stop talking in riddles, what do you mean?"

"Right, let's stop talking in riddles, let me give it to you straight, you are a worthless drunk!" roared Jefferson.

Michael stared at the two agents blankly. "What?"

"Oh, please Michael, don't even try to lie, I can smell it on you!"

Michael sniffed his shirt and in an instant, he realized what had happened. "Look, this is a misunderstanding, I..."

Jefferson cut in and said, "Listen to me Michael, we don't have time to listen to any more lies right now, so just sit tight and let us do our job."

Michael got up and said, "It's my job too!"

"No Michael, *it was*," saying this Jefferson stormed out of the room.

Michael looked at Sam with pleading eyes. "Please Sam, you have to believe me!"

"Rest assured, I won't make *that* mistake again."

Sam hurried out of the room to catch up with Jefferson, who was on his way to have a word with the captain. They had no time to spare, as Oliver already had a substantial lead, the only chance they had was to determine the direction Oliver had taken, and then call for backup. Jefferson had a cursory discussion with the captain as to what to do. Apart from finding a way to track Oliver, the major problem was to calm the other passengers, who were still clueless as to the true nature of the situation. Jefferson went to the announcement microphone and quickly explained the events that had transpired. Most of the passengers gave looks of surprise but fortunately, the confusion subsided.

The first order which Jefferson gave was to head back towards NYC at the earliest, there was no sense in staying disconnected from the land anymore. Oliver had escaped but he had to be tracked and they could not do that while on a cruise ship. While the captain gave sharp orders to alter the course of the ship, Jefferson talked to Sam about the situation Michael found himself in. Both of them were infuriated with what Michael had done, they felt that their trust had been misused and that made them want to make Michael pay for what he had done, but a career in law enforcement instilled a habit in one's nature – to listen to what the guilty party had to say. Thus, while the captain and the crew tried to shed some further light on Oliver's actions and steer the ship back towards NYC, Sam and Jefferson decided to have a talk with Michael.

Michael was still where they had left him, in Oliver's cabin, but he was delighted to see that the agents were back, even more so when he realized that they wanted to hear his side of the story. Michael began from the time he had woken up during the night, to the time he had been knocked out by Oliver. He explained each and every incident in the clearest manner and by the time he was done, the agents knew what had happened as though they had been there themselves. But the precise manner in which Michael narrated the chain of events did not mean that the two agents believed him. They could believe everything, from Michael discovering the clue, to Michael getting beaten up, but what they doubted was whether he had really been drugged by Oliver or not.

"So, you mean Oliver tricked you?" asked Sam.

"He did, he drugged me!"

"You say he did it while you two were in the bar?" asked Jefferson.

"Yes, why?" asked Michael with a hint of uncertainty in his voice.

"We would have seen him on the CCTV."

"You think he couldn't drug a man in a way that it isn't visible in the footage? You know as well as I do what he is capable of!"

"If what you say is true, then the bartender would have seen Oliver do something odd," said Jefferson and motioned Michael towards the door.

A minute later, the three agents were standing in the bar and the bartender was facing them. He corroborated the entire conversation that Michael had with Oliver, but when questioned by the agents regarding the drug, he seemed to be clueless.

"Added something? What do you mean?"

"Did you see Oliv...Gary slip any drug in Michael's drink?" asked Jefferson.

"Who's Michael?"

"He means John," added Sam.

The bartender thought for a minute. "Nope, didn't see anything."

"What do you mean you didn't see anything? You were here the entire time!" shouted Michael.

"That's right, I was here the entire time," agreed the bartender. "But I did not see Gary slip anything into your lemonade."

Michael was about to say something else when Jefferson said, "I think that will be all."

"No!" exclaimed Michael. "Look, the walls of the cabins are not soundproof, and Oliver and I were not exactly whispering, the person in the neighboring cabin must have heard something!"

Jefferson looked at Sam and the latter raised an eyebrow to which the former responded with a nod of the head. Five minutes later, Jefferson and Sam were talking to the person who occupied the cabin towards the right of Oliver's. Michael had been asked to remain in his cabin while the two agents did the questioning, and Michael had responded to this order with a look of agony.

Will Singer lit a cigarette and said, "You don't mind if I smoke, do you?"

"We'd prefer if you didn't," said Jefferson.

"So, what did you want to talk to me about?" asked Will ignoring what Jefferson had said.

"Were you in your room between half past one and four in the morning?"

"Of course, where else would I be?"

"Did you happen to hear anything?"

Will gave an odd expression. "What do you mean?"

Jefferson looked at Sam. The man was clearly hiding something.

"Did you hear two people conversing?"

"Maybe, depends on which people you are referring to."

"How many people did you hear?"

"Two."

"Then that's the pair we are talking about."

"Fine. I did hear voices."

"And what were they talking about?"

"Oh, you know what I recorded the entire conversation, but I just left the tape at my cabin," said Will with a hint of sarcasm in his voice.

"We don't want any nonsense, just tell us what you heard."

"What's in it for me?"

Jefferson was about to reply when he remembered something. Michael believed that the man had some unlawful business going on, maybe smuggling. He decided to take a shot in the dark.

"Tell us what you know and perhaps we will be lenient with you on the smuggling matter."

The smile vanished from Will's face instantly. "What do you mean?"

"You know what I mean, and also I wanted to tell you that we are FBI agents." Said Jefferson as he and Sam showed the man their identification.

Will exhaled a puff of smoke. "I did hear Gary and another man talking, they seemed to be having an argument of some sort, then there were some thuds, like a fight and then there was silence, until the alarms started blaring."

Jefferson looked at Will for a moment before saying, "What exactly did you hear?"

"There was something about diamonds and chess and a name... I think it was Oliver."

Jefferson was silent, and so was Sam. Michael's story corroborated exactly with what Will was telling them, and that was an indication that Michael was telling the truth, at least as far as the conversation was concerned.

"Very well, you may go," said Jefferson

Will got up, did a mock salute, and then left.

"So, do you believe Michael?" asked Sam.

"I believe that he is telling the truth regarding the conversation he had with Oliver."

"And about his drinking?"

"I find it hard to believe that he didn't drink. Maybe he was able to resist but I'm not sure, what I'm sure of is that I don't trust him anymore."

"And what does that mean for him?"

Jefferson did not reply. He didn't know what to do anymore, Oliver was gone, Michael had disappointed him, and they had no further leads on the case. They didn't even know who Oliver intended to sell the diamonds to.

Suddenly the door of the lounge opened, and Michael entered. His face was pale, and his forehead was beaded with sweat. He looked at Jefferson and then at Sam.

"Well? What did Will tell you?"

Jefferson did not reply. He stood up, and Sam followed.

Jefferson said, "Michael, hand in your resignation by tomorrow."

Jefferson did not look at either of the people standing in front of him, and he exited, leaving behind two astounded young men.

CHAPTER TWENTY-EIGHT

FBI field office, NYC:

Jefferson was sitting in his office with a letter in his hand. It was Michael's letter of resignation. After Jefferson had asked Michael to hand in his resignation, Michael was distraught, he had pleaded with Jefferson not to do this to him, to trust him, but Jefferson could not. In the end, he had to threaten Michael, saying that if he didn't resign of his own will, he would fire him anyway, and that would be a much less respectable business. Michael had looked at him with such hate that Jefferson was shocked. He had been expecting bitterness, but what Michael displayed was hate so intense, that Jefferson felt compelled to get away from him. The next day, Michael had handed in his resignation letter and today, he would be coming to empty his cubicle.

Suddenly Jefferson's phone rang, the call was from security to ask for authorization to let Michael enter the building. Jefferson gave the required permission and after a few minutes, Michael entered the bullpen. Instead of formal attire, Michael was dressed in jeans, a t-shirt and a coat. This was a sign that he had accepted that he was a civilian now. Nobody in the bullpen wanted to make eye contact with him. Only Sam made a futile attempt to talk to him.

"Hello, Michael."

Instead of replying, Michael walked past him as though he didn't exist. Sam's cheeks flushed and he went to his cubicle. After five minutes, Michael exited the cubicle which used to be his, with a small cardboard box in his hand. Jefferson came out of his office and walked up to Michael.

"Michael, I..."

But before he could complete his sentence, Michael took his leave. Jefferson looked at Michael as he left, thinking about the decision he had made and whether it was a mistake.

Michael's Apartment:

Michael was sitting on the floor of his apartment with a black backpack beside him. The apartment consisted of furniture, but there were no clothes in the almirah and no personal effects in the drawers. Michael had packed up everything and his luggage had been sent ahead the previous day. The reason for this action was that he had decided to shift. He was leaving behind the part of his life that had passed and he could not stay in the same place where he had lived when he was an agent. The memories brought up an odd mix of emotions which were not healthy for Michael. In a short course of time, his life had changed and thus, he had to change his surroundings as well.

Michael stood up and looked at his wristwatch. It was time. He picked up the bag and didn't even look back once as he went out the door.

After managing to get a cab, he had to force himself to do the one thing which he had been dreading to do for a long time. He didn't even want to think about it, but he felt that it was unavoidable to deal with it.

After what felt like just a few moments, Michael was standing outside Evelyn's door, unsure about how to proceed. Finally, he mustered up courage and rang the doorbell. Evelyn opened the door and Michael was greeted by the usual "Who is it?" in Rob's voice, coming from the living room.

"Hello, Michael."

"Hello, Evelyn."

She moved aside to let him enter and he did, although nervously. Rob was also in the room, and he perked up when he saw who their guest was.

"Michael!"

"Hello Rob, how are you?"

"Perfectly fine, other than the fact that my sister is forcing me to complete my homework, so thinking about it, I don't feel very well."

Michael laughed. Evelyn said, "Rob why don't you finish your homework inside? So that you can concentrate."

Rob got up and said, "I don't want to concentrate," but he went in, nonetheless.

"So, how are you, Michael?"

"Evelyn I'm here to talk about something very important."

"What is it?"

"I don't think it's a good idea for us to be friends anymore."

"What? What Happened?"

Evelyn was shocked and there was no need to be a behavioral analyst to know that. Her eyes had widened, and her cheeks had paled.

"Something happened, Evelyn, and I'm in a place in my life where I don't want any friends," said Michael with a very heavy heart. This was far more difficult than he had expected.

"Michael, whatever it is we can talk about it. Is this because the robber got away?"

Michael knew how she was aware of what had happened. Everyone had seen the news, the news where the reporters were announcing the failure of the FBI.

"Please Evelyn, this is very difficult as it is, don't make it worse," said Michael in a heavy voice.

Evelyn was finding it hard to maintain her composure, but she said, "All right Michael. It was good to have a friend like you."

Michael got up. "Believe me, the feeling is likewise."

He exited the apartment in a hurry as he felt that if he stayed in the apartment any longer, he would not be able to sever his connections with Evelyn, and that was something which had to be done. He had no choice.

Michael got in a cab and gave his destination as a specific bookstore. He had no work in the bookstore, but he had his reasons for wanting to go there, reasons which were very personal. After some time, he reached his destination and went into the bookstore. He had to wait for some time and thus, picked up a book and pretended to read it while his eyes were focused on his watch. At the right time, he closed the book, replaced it on the shelf and exited the bookstore. He then walked for some time until he reached a run-down warehouse. He opened the look at the door with a key from his pocket and closed the door behind him as he entered. The sunlight filtered through the newspaper-covered windows and Michael squinted to see clearly around him. There was dust everywhere, but through the dust, one could see a faint glimmer of light on the back end of the warehouse.

Suddenly, someone addressed Michael, "Took you long enough to come here."

Michael whirled around as the figure of a man emerged from the shadows. They both stared at each other with intense expressions. The man was the person who was responsible for Michael losing his job, he was the man who had manipulated the FBI, and the man was Oliver.

A moment later, Oliver and Michael laughed at the same time and then gave each other a high five as though they were brothers.

CHAPTER TWENTY-NINE

Four days later, an island at unknown nautical coordinates:

Rain was falling from the sky in sheets and the sea was on a high tide. The soft patter of the raindrops was contrasted and yet complemented by the loud noise made by the crashing waves. Michael was standing on the balcony of a large and beautifully built house which faced towards the sea. He had a cup of coffee in his hand, and looked around him with an air of authority, as though he owned the place, which was absolutely true. He was the owner of a large chunk of the lush green, tropical island where the house was situated. This ownership was a legacy left behind by his parents, a legacy that he was carrying forward. The only other inhabitants of the island were tribals whose association with the family had been since they had first bought the island, generations ago, and permitted the tribals to live as they had been living since before the island came into the possession of Michael's family. This act had touched the hearts of the tribals, and they had begun to see the family as a part of their own group. Michael looked different now, very different. His medium-length hair was combed with style, his beard was trimmed into a neat French cut and his eyes were shining. Gone was the man with the ruffled hair, tired manner and exhausted looks, the alcohol addict. The man who now stood on the balcony of the house was the definition of a smart personality.

Michael was staring at the waves when suddenly, his attention was caught by the sound of someone entering the large sitting room behind him. Two people had entered the sitting room and they sat down on the comfortable couch. Michael walked in and sat on the large armchair facing the two people. He smiled a little.

He placed the now empty cup of coffee on the table and addressing the other occupants of the room, he said, "You obviously have a lot of questions and rest assured, all of them will be answered, the only condition is that you listen to what I am about to tell you with rapt attention and without any interruptions. By the end, you will know it all and it will leave you dumbstruck."

The two looked at Michael with wide eyes, as though they could not believe what they were seeing.

Michael noticed their surprise and laughed a little. "Come on! Don't look so surprised, although I do admit, I saved the ring thieves from the FBI."

Indeed, the two people who were seated in front of Michael were none other than Brandon and Olivia, the ring thieves, who had been presumed dead by the entire world.

"Michael? You...You did this?" asked Olivia.

"But you're a fed!" exclaimed Brandon.

"Answering your questions chronologically – yes and no. Yes, I planned it, all of it, although I didn't execute the plan alone and no, I'm not an FBI agent, not anymore."

Michael interlaced his fingers. "Now, as I promised, I would tell you everything, but you would have to be patient."

"Well, start already!" said Brandon.

"One moment, there is one other person whose presence is currently required," said Michael, and then raised his voice and said, "Come on in!"

After a moment, a man walked into the room. Motioning towards the man with his arm, Michael said, "Allow me to introduce you to Walter, or as you know him, Oliver."

The man who had walked in gave a lopsided smile as he looked at the stunned faces of Olivia and Brandon.

"Oliver had kidnapped us, you...you aren't Oliver," said Olivia.

And it was true, the physical appearance of Walter had changed dramatically. His eyes were now sea green instead of the ordinary brown that they used to be, he did not wear spectacles, and the color of his skin was much lighter. He was clean-shaven and even his hairstyle was different, now it was relatively shorter than before, and the shade was halfway between brown and black.

Walter laughed, a carefree and childlike laugh. "I know! I'm not the same person, at least I don't *look* the same, it's all the magic of makeup."

"What do you mean?" asked Brandon.

Michael interrupted and said, "Relax, all questions will be answered in due time. Now, let's start at the beginning, shall we?"

And thus, Michael began his narrative, a narrative, the likes of which no one had ever heard before.

"To state the obvious, I was the one who planned all of it. Committing the heists, getting you out of prison, every single thing. I have been planning all of this for years, since a long time before I even joined the FBI. In fact, my true motive behind becoming an FBI agent was to work with Jefferson Brown. There were two reasons for the same, the first was to observe him, to scrutinize him psychologically as well as physically to understand how he reacts in situations and what his probable moves are, I had started profiling him even before joining the FBI, I analyzed each decision he took, each emotion he expressed and each order he gave but I was able to do this much better when I worked alongside him. The second reason was that I always needed to be two steps ahead of the FBI, I wanted them to do what I wanted, and I did not want any surprises. The easiest way to achieve this was if I was working the case alongside Jefferson Brown. I don't like praising my opponents, but it would be unwise to ignore the fact that the FBI are quite good at what they do and I was able to manipulate the situation to my advantage at all times only because they did not know that the man they were after was the man they were sharing their plans with.

For years, I perfected every step of the plan by running simulations in my head until I felt nothing could go wrong. That was when I joined the FBI. My plan did not involve me making any moves in the first two years working with Jefferson because I had to gain their trust and thus, I had plenty of time to work on the second stage of my plan."

"Which was?" prompted Brandon.

"Finding a partner," said Michael. "I needed someone whom I could trust with my life, someone who was smart enough to be able to outwit the FBI and yet it had to be someone who was not even remotely associated with me. That was when I tracked down a person who was practically a ghost - Walter. He was the one person who fit all the criteria and whom I could trust, whom I do trust, as I would trust my brother. He was to play a pivotal part in the plan, and that part was the part of Oliver. He would be the one committing the robberies based on the plan I had made; he would be the mastermind of the plan in the eyes of the authorities. Next, I needed to find a partner for Oliver. You see, perfect as the plan was, I couldn't risk the FBI discovering Oliver's true identity, thus he was to change his appearance at all times through make-up and also, he needed someone who could be the face of the duo and make contact with the people whose services we required so that when the FBI pieced together the clues I wanted them to, and followed the trail, the identity they would uncover would be the identity of the expendable person."

"Calvin," muttered Olivia.

"Precisely. Glad to see you are catching on. I could not just choose any person for that job, it was a job that involved a considerable risk, the risk of death. So, I researched to find the dirtiest and most horrible criminal I could find, someone who would not be mourned nor remembered rather, people would be glad to get rid of him. I found that person in Calvin, he was involved in nearly all the crimes which are committed by people who have no moral, supplying drugs, even to minors, extortion, kidnapping, torture and multiple murders, that was Calvin's resume. He had been arrested and he had got the chair, but he escaped during prison transfer. He was the perfect candidate for the job and thus he became Oliver's partner."

"And then they stole the diamonds," said Olivia.

"Not quite. There were still two things to be done. Did you hear about the robbery in the London art gallery, over an year ago?"

Brandon's eyes went wide. "You were the one who stole the paintings?"

"Yes, to carry out the plan, I needed funds and those could not be obtained in any legal way and thus I planned and committed the robbery. At that time, I could not take the risk of Walter getting exposed, which is why, I did it myself. Took an off from work saying that my parents were relocating, which was partially true, because they already had relocated, but still, I went and committed the crime, sold the paintings, and thus obtained the necessary funds for the job."

Brandon nodded approvingly, "That was smart, committing a robbery to finance a robbery."

"*Merci,*" said Michael in a perfect accent.

Olivia said, "You said that there were two things, what was the other one?"

"I had to portray myself as an alcohol addict. It was hard, since I detest alcohol, and as far as I can remember, there have been only five occasions when I have actually ingested alcohol but I had to make the others believe it so I began acting as though I had the same signs, I used to keep myself awake at night to make sure that I looked the part, then there were a few actions and *voila*, I was an alcoholic. I let this continue for another year, when I realized that all the pieces were in their correct positions, and it was time to bring the plan in action."

"So, you committed the first heist, *Les morceaux de Lumiere*," said Olivia.

"No, *they* committed the first heist," said Michael motioning towards Walter "And it all went well, now, you know how we committed it so I won't waste time repeating that, but everyone was surprised as to how the thieves managed to get the thumbprint, the truth is that it was my doing. I had secretly picked up the glass which David was using for his drink, and I safely kept it in the bag that I was carrying. And I was also the one who had suggested that they get an extra guard so that Calvin could impersonate him and gain access."

"And I got the print from the glass and converted it to a synthetic and reusable form," said Walter.

Olivia shook her head sadly and said, "That is what Claire used to do."

Walter looked at her oddly, but he did not say anything.

Michael shot a glance towards Walter and then continued, "Now, the fun part was the car. I had to inform Jefferson about the next robbery and humiliate him at the same time so, through my contacts, I got the car registered to a shell corporation but instead of giving a dummy address, I gave the agents the address of the location I wanted them to go to."

"That was where you had spray painted the Rafool Edmunds thing," said Brandon.

"Exactly. In fact, I was the one who had suggested that we follow the paint clue so that we could obtain the face of one of the thieves, Calvin. That was where you came in Brandon, and I must say, that was a splendid sketch you drew."

"Thanks."

"Moving on, the only clue I gave the agents was that we were going to rob Harold Williamson's collection next. My plan centered on causing as much of a stir as possible, I realized what better way to gain attention than exposing that the son of a well-known millionaire possesses a valuable and illegal collection and then steal it. And it worked, although Jefferson kept it quiet at the beginning, which was something unexpected, but still, I never said he wasn't smart, but my goal was the source of my profound motivation."

"And you succeeded, you managed to steal the collection," said Brandon with a hint of admiration in his voice.

"We did. We used Calvin as a distraction, while Walter conveniently stole the collection. Getting him in the venue was a bit of a snag as it had to be done without pointing any suspicion towards me, but I gave cover to Walter as he caused the little riot and entered the property," said Michael with a little smile.

"And then Walter kidnapped us," said Olivia.

"Yep, he kidnapped you and then broadcasted an edited video as a live feed to fool the world and make them believe that you had died while you had just been knocked unconscious by darts. He is very gifted with computers, he can do anything and everything with technology, that is how he edited the video with such perfection that everyone believed it, even the so-called video experts."

"And then you got us here and kept us as prisoners," said Olivia.

"It had to be done, it was for your own good."

Brandon looked at Michael with a raised eyebrow, "For our own good? Care to elaborate? We are in the dark here."

"You have been watching the news."

"But that only tells us that you got away with the diamonds, that doesn't tell us what happened."

"All in good time," said Walter.

"You don't get to shut us up, not anymore, you kidnapped us! Who do you think you are?" asked an enraged Olivia.

Michael looked at Walter and a silent understanding seemed to pass between the two. It was time.

Walter said, "I'm Claire's son."

CHAPTER THIRTY

Brandon and Olivia were stunned, they could not speak, they could only stare. Both of them were staring at Walter as though they were seeing him for the first time.

Walter looked at them and said, "Hello Uncle Brandon, Hello Aunt Olivia."

Olivia rushed forwards and hugged Walter, and Brandon did the same. They ruffled Walter's hair as though he was still a little child. Michael was looking at the trio with a wide smile on his face.

Walter said, "And you know what? Michael here..."

"...is going to tell you the rest of the story when you're done," interjected Michael and looked at Walter. Walter gave Michael a quizzical look, but Michael just gave slight nod of his head as if to say – "everything in due time.". Walter understood and he said no more.

Once Brandon and Olivia were seated once again and had forced Walter to sit beside them, Michael continued. He told them the events which had taken place on the ship, but Brandon and Olivia still had questions.

"So, who was the person you were going to sell the diamonds to?"

Michael laughed and said, "Don't you get it? There was no one there to buy the diamonds, it was just something that the FBI was made to believe."

"But if you told Walter what was going on, that the captain's diamond was fake, then why would he check the diamonds and get his footage on the camera?"

"Did you really think that after all we had done, we would be stupid enough to let ourselves get taped on CCTV? No, he inspected the diamonds in the camera to make sure that he was recorded. There had to be some proof for me as well as the other agents to see."

"But then why did you two fight each other?"

"To make Will hear the sounds which he did, so that the agents could not even guess that the two of us were a team," and then turning towards Walter he said, "oh and, by the way, you didn't pull your punches."

Walter gave a slight smile and said, "Was I supposed to? I thought we had to stick to the plan and make it as realistic as possible."

"Very funny."

Suddenly Brandon realized something. "So that means Walter didn't drug you in the bar, that's why the bartender did not see anything!"

"That's correct," said Walter.

"Yep, I just took a little tablet afterwards to knock myself out," said Michael.

"But why did he sprinkle alcohol on you?" asked Olivia.

"I must admit, I asked him to do that for entirely selfish reasons, I had to quit the FBI because my job was done, but I couldn't just resign without a reason, given the circumstances, it would have seemed suspicious, so I got Jefferson to ask me to leave."

"Brilliant!" exclaimed Olivia.

"The perfect Plan" commented Brandon.

"Thank you very much, coming from the best thieves of their time, it means a lot?"

"Of their time?" asked Olivia with a smile.

Walter laughed and Michael said, "Oh, I think you will agree you've got some competition now."

Once the laughter had died down, Olivia realized something. There were things that didn't make sense.

With a confused expression on her face, she said, "Wait a minute, you said *you* found Walter, that all of it was *your* plan."

"Yes, what's your point?" asked Michael but he knew exactly what her point was.

"My point is, why would you plan to get us out? Why would you plan to humiliate Jefferson? Why in the world would you specifically target *Les morceaux De Lumiere*?"

Michael's face went slack. He was feeling nervous, and he didn't want to admit it, but he was scared. He had feared this moment since he was thirteen, he was unsure of how to proceed, and he was at a loss for words. This time it was Walter who came to his rescue.

"It's all right Michael, it's time. Tell them."

"Tell us what?" asked Brandon.

"The truth," said Michael. His heart seemed to skip a beat, but he could feel his pulse quickening, his hands were cold and for the first time in his life, he felt butterflies in his stomach.

"Tell us what Michael?" repeated Olivia.

Michael got up and went and sat down near the couple's feet. They started, but they were too stunned to move after seeing the expression on Michael's face. Michael's eyes were filled with tears and his voice was quivering, but when he spoke, he expressed all his emotions with each word that escaped his lips.

"It is time for me to tell you the truth," said Michael. "And the truth is, I'm your son."

CHAPTER THIRTY-ONE

Olivia and Brandon were dumbfounded. They were feeling so many emotions at the same time that they couldn't decide what to do. They wanted to cry, they wanted to rejoice, they wanted to shout to the world that they were with their son, but they also wanted to spend all their time with him, just with him.

Finally, Olivia found her voice, tears flowing freely, she said, "You...are...you are my son, *our* son?"

Michael took her hand and placing it on his cheek, which was moist from tears, he said, "Yes, yes! Mom, dad, I...I'm your son, I am your son!"

His father was sobbing but all he could do was hug his son, his mother kept kissing him on the head and hugging him. They had lost hope of ever seeing their son again, but now, here he was right in front of them, and it did not even cross their mind that Michael could be telling a lie, they knew it was true, they knew like a parent knows their child.

After some minutes, the three of them calmed down a little, but Brandon and Olivia were still gripping Michael as they would never let him go again, never ever. There was a wide smile on Michael's face, and he looked happier than he had ever looked before, and the same was the case with his feelings.

Walter said, "Aren't you guys a little confused? I mean, when Michael told me who he was, even I was confused."

Olivia nodded and looking at her son, she said, "How did you do this?"

"And how did you get in the FBI? They must have done an extensive background check," said Brandon.

Michael got up and said, "For that, we would be requiring the presence of three other people in the room."

Michael picked up a small phone from the side table and pressed a button. After a moment he spoke up, "Yes, I told them, come on in."

Olivia and Brandon were confused, but all their question were answered as soon as another couple, of the same age as they were, entered the room along with a girl who was just a few years younger than Michael. The man had his gray hair cut very short, and his eyes were twinkling, and seemed to be smiling, just as his lips were. Out of the two women, the elder one had long, red hair and was clutching a handkerchief, while the younger woman had her red hair cut a little shorter than shoulder length and her hazel eyes were eagerly looking towards each member of the room. Each of the new arrivals was tanned as though they had recently spent quite a lot of time on a beach.

Olivia's eyes went wide, "Jasmine? Frank?"

Brandon looked at them and said, "So you kept your promise."

"We did," said Frank in his deep voice.

Jasmine hugged Olivia and said, "How could we not? You're family."

Michael said, "I guess you guys must have understood most of it by now, but still, let me surmise it for everyone's sake."

Everyone sat in the room and looked intently at Michael. When viewed as a whole, they looked like a big, happy family, one that was not bound by blood but by their affection for each other.

Michael began, "Till my thirteenth birthday, my life was very simple, Aunt Jasmine and Uncle Frank were my parents, Mary was my younger sister, and we were a happy family, but everything changed on the morning of my thirteenth birthday. Frank and Jasmine decided that I was mature enough to understand the truth and thus, they saw it as their duty to tell me who I really was. They told me that I was the son of the famous ring thieves and that they were the closest friends of my parents. They told me that my parents wanted to retire but before they could do that, they had to do one last job, but before they could pull it off, I was born. My mother and father decided that it was not safe for them to raise me until they were retired as they led a life which had no place for a child, and it was true. So, with a heavy heart, they made an arrangement with their best friends. To make sure that if something happened to them, no one would ever know who I was, they left me at an orphanage and according to the arrangement their best friends had agreed to adopt me the very next day and raise me as their very own son, which they did." At this point Michael paused.

All the inhabitants of the room were trying very hard not to let their tears escape their eyes but most of them failed. Olivia and Jasmine were sitting together with their arms around each other to provide support, physical and emotional. Brandon and Frank were staring into space, while Walter and Mary were looking at Michael.

After taking a sip of water, Michael continued, "The arrangement which was supposed to be temporary turned into permanent when a young FBI agent successfully captured my parents and destroyed my life. Naturally, I did not believe any of it at first, but it was only when Aunt

Jasmine swore on my life, that I realized that what they had said was absolutely true. From that day, there was only one goal in my life - to get my parents out and make Jefferson Brown pay for what he did. So, from the age of thirteen years, I began formulating my plan, and after *years*, I was able to bring to a successful conclusion and I ended up the luckiest man in the world, with not one but two mothers, two fathers, the best sister and a friend who is closer to me than a brother could have ever been."

This time, no one made any attempt to suppress their tears, but this time they were tears of pure joy and happiness.

After some time, All the members of the family were seated around a large table, enjoying a splendid meal, prepared by their chef, who was a member of the local tribe which called the island their home. The chef was not trained like the chefs in metropolitan cities, but he had the gift of preparing the most delicious meals from the simplest of ingredients and thus, on that day, he had presented the inhabitants of the house with a sample of his brilliant culinary skills. Everyone laughed and talked freely, with their hearts full of peace and their minds thinking of nothing else but the conversation they were having. Frank and Jasmine were telling Brandon and Olivia stories of Michael and Mary when they were children, while Michael, Walter, and Mary were talking about how the plan had turned out to be perfect.

"Who did you sell the diamonds to?" asked Walter. "You didn't even tell *me*."

"Yes, who was the buyer?" asked Mary. "From the looks of it, he paid you quite a good price."

Michael smiled and said, "I haven't sold the diamonds yet, and I don't plan to."

"Then where are they?" asked Mary.

"Just watch," said Michael as a butler entered the room with a large dish.

"Oh, I don't think I can eat any more food!" exclaimed Olivia with a laugh.

The butler placed the dish in the center of the table and removed the cover.

Everyone except Michael gasped.

"They're beautiful!" exclaimed Mary.

Indeed, they were, because sitting in the center of the plate were four of the diamonds, two in the form of pendants and the other two in the form of bracelets. Each piece of jewelry had a name tag attached to it. The four name tags read – Olivia, Brandon, Jasmine, and Frank.

Michael stood up and said, "That is a gift from my side to my parents, the people to whom I owe my life!"

Everyone's eyes were moist as the ladies wore the pendants and the men proudly wore the bracelets.

"They are the diamonds that you wanted and now, they are in your possession. They are the diamonds that started this, it is only fitting to bring them in at the end," said Michael.

All the others were speechless. Their emotions were so strong that they were unable to find any words to express them.

After a moment, it was Walter who spoke up. "But what about the fifth diamond?"

Michael smiled sadly and said, "Well, I gifted four to my parents, but you didn't think I would not get a souvenir for another important person who is not here today?"

"Who?" asked Mary.

Michael reached into the pocket of his pants and extracted a small box. In the center of the box rested the fifth diamond.

Picking up the diamond, Michael turned to Walter and said, "This is for Aunt Claire, as a tribute to her talent and loyalty."

Walter took the diamond and looked at Michael with grateful eyes. For a few moments, everyone at the table was silent.

Suddenly Mary turned to Michael and said, "But if the diamonds are here, then where did you get the money from?"

"Well, I did not sell the diamonds, which is obvious, but you are forgetting about the collection," said Michael. "It contained priceless elements from the animal kingdom, skins, ivory, you name it. It was more than enough to get me a fortune."

Everyone at the table had a smile on their lips, after all, each one of them was a practitioner of the art of deception and deceit, and to witness such a brilliant performance of the same was a rare privilege.

Mary said, "You could have made some more money, Michael."

"How?" asked Michael.

"By forging the diamonds and selling them to even more people! Everyone would have thought that they were in possession of the original collection, and I could have easily forged the diamonds, I'm quite good, you know."

"I never doubted your ability for a moment! You are the best, no doubt," explained Michael. "But the diamonds are unique, it is impossible to get a forgery that would mirror all their qualities."

"We'll see," said Mary.

"Oh, cheer up! all that we have to do now is have fun! We are free, we can go where we want, do what we want, and live a peaceful life," said Michael as he ran an eye along the people who were seated at the table, his family.

Mary gave Michael a wide smile and once again, the conversion shifted to different channels. When one is happy, one is tempted to talk a lot, and that was what was going on, no one wanted this time to come to an end. They had been separated and unhappy for too long, now was their time to enjoy life.

While the youngsters were in the middle of a conversation on one end of the table, the senior members of the family were discussing something in very serious tones.

Olivia said, "How can we ever repay you for what you have done?"

"There is no need to repay us, as I said before, you are family," replied Jasmine.

"And there is no need for the phrase 'Thank You' in a family," added Frank with a warm smile.

Brandon just kept a hand on Frank's shoulder, but no words escaped his lips.

After a moment, Jasmine said, "Do you remember you left something else for us when we had parted?"

Brandon said, "How can we forget, the collection of all of the most valuable items we robbed over the course of our entire career."

"Correct, all safely stashed away in a locker. Rest assured, it is as you had left it, we made sure of that," stated Frank.

"But you could have used it! Sold it! Michael could have used the money in his plan!" exclaimed Olivia.

"We would never even think of using it without your permission first, you had left it so that we would keep it safe, not use it," said Jasmine.

"And as for the question of letting Michael use it, we wouldn't lie, that thought had crossed our minds but, in the end, we decided that it was your possession and we had no right to pass it on, even if it was to your son," said Frank.

Brandon and Olivia looked at the couple seated in front of them with grateful eyes. Here were two people who understood the meaning of true friendship and practiced it with utmost devotion. They were the kind of people who proved to be invaluable to anyone they ever formed an association with, and they had just proved the same by their actions so far.

Olivia said, "You call yourself our family and then divide the possessions? Remember, what is ours is yours, always was and always will be."

Now it was Frank and Jasmine's turn to look grateful. No words were exchanged, all the emotions were conveyed by the expressions of the two couples.

On the other end of the table, Mary had just remembered something.

She said, "So what about your friend, does she know?"

Walter looked surprised, "What friend?"

Michael said, "Oh, nobody."

"Nobody?" exclaimed Mary in surprise. "She was the only person you referred to as a 'friend' apart from Walter, and believe me, you have a serious lack of friends in your life."

"So, what's the name of your special friend?" asked Walter.

"Just friend and her name is Evelyn Watson."

"And who's Evelyn Watson?" asked Walter.

"Like I said, Michael's special friend," said Mary.

Michael's face turned serious, and he said, "I admit she was the only unexpected thing in the plan, the only variable

I hadn't accounted for - romantic attraction."

"So, what happened?" asked Mary.

"I had to end it. I couldn't afford to have anyone close to me, it was far too dangerous for me as well as for her. I couldn't risk the plan for just my feelings."

Mary looked at her brother with admiration. Placing her hand on his arm, she said, "I'm proud of you, Michael."

Walter said, "And I am thankful to you, for giving me a family again."

Michael gave them both a warm smile, but he was thinking about the last gift he had left for Evelyn.

Evelyn's Apartment:

Evelyn could not help but think about Michael. She tried to focus on other things, but her memories with Michael were far more pleasant than what was in front of her. She was reading a letter from the owner of the apartment, stating that she had to pay the rent as soon as possible as her previous month's rent was also pending.

Rob came over and sat down beside her. He was smiling and there was a bulge in his pocket. Evelyn looked at him and smiled.

"What are you so happy about?"

"I have a gift for you."

"What?"

Rob got a small pouch from his pocket and emptied its contents onto the table. After he was done, a small pile of coins and a few notes were lying on the table.

"I saw that you had to pay the bill, so here is my contribution," said Rob with pride.

Evelyn could not help but smile. "But this is too much!"

Rob nodded his head, "Even I thought so! Here, let me take back five dollars, and you can use the rest of it to pay some rent in advance."

"That's a brilliant idea!"

Rob smiled widely, kissed his sister on the cheek and ran into his room, feeling very proud of himself.

Suddenly, Evelyn's phone rang. The call was from the bank and worry lines creased Evelyn's forehead at once. Getting a call from the bank almost never meant good news. But as soon as Evelyn heard what the woman from the bank had to say, she could feel her legs trembling from shock and her heart singing with joy. Her hands were shaking and yet, her lips were smiling.

The woman from the bank had said, "Ma'am there has been a transfer to your account. The amount is..."

To put it in an informal manner, the amount of money which had been transferred made Evelyn feel that she was the owner of a fortune.

CHAPTER THIRTY-TWO

The Federal building, NYC:

Jefferson was seated in his office when Sam walked in with a concerned expression on his face.

"What's the matter?" asked Jefferson.

"Jefferson, I just wanted to see how you were doing," said Sam.

"I'm perfectly all right, I've got a case to work on and so do you."

"What case?"

"We need to catch Oliver."

"Jefferson..." began Sam.

"No, Sam, I won't let anyone get away with something like that, he thinks he has won the game, but he mistakes the triumph of a round for winning the game."

"Do we have any leads?"

"Yep, I've got Gary's photo," said Jefferson.

"Gary?"

"Oliver's alias, and that means, we have Oliver's photo."

Sam had a glint in his eyes. "So, what's the beginning point of our investigation?"

Jefferson "Let's look into the files, find one, and then let's get him. I know I won't rest until I do, what about you?"

Sam looked determined when he said, "I'll get the files."

As Sam exited the office, Jefferson looked at the note that Oliver had sent him, the first one, about the robbery of the diamonds.

There was motivation in Jefferson's voice as he said, "Wherever you are, I'm coming to get you."

The Island:

Michael was standing outside the living room with a worried expression on his face. Although what he was seeing made him happy, what he was thinking about made him concerned. He saw that Jasmine, Frank and Mary were showing Michael and Mary's childhood photos to Brandon and Olivia. There was a question which had been troubling Michael for a long time, and the answer to the question had chances of being a threat to the happiness which Michael had found with his family.

Walter came over and stood beside Michael. "It's quite peaceful, isn't it? knowing that everything is all right now."

"I hope so."

Walter looked at Michael and said, "What do you mean?"

"Did you send me any messages?"

"What sort of messages?"

In reply, Michael took out an envelope from his pocket and handed it to Walter. Walter opened it and took out its contents. It contained the chits of paper on which the messages Michael had received were printed.

Walter's eyes widened. "What does this mean? Who sent you these?"

Michael stared at his family and varied thoughts ran in his mind as he said, "Those are the questions we need to find answers to."

Michael's Former Apartment:

It was late night, and a man was walking around in Michael's former apartment. He was checking each and every corner, but without even making a single sound. Even if a person was standing with his ear pressed to the door, they would not have known that there was someone inside the apartment, and this was to be expected from the man, he was a professional. The man had a mini camera fitted into his glasses and the video was being broadcasted live to another location.

After a moment, the man raised his hand and touching the communication device on one of his ears, he said, "Sir, there is nothing here."

Far away, a man was sitting in a dark room, and his eyes were focused on a computer kept on the desk in front of him. As soon as the voice of the man in Michael's apartment blared through a Bluetooth speaker on the table, the man banged his fist on the desk.

"What do you mean there is nothing? Where did he go?"

"Sir, there is no clue here, it appears he has just vanished."

"Where would he go on such a short notice?"

"I don't know sir."

"I wasn't talking to you."

"My apologies sir."

"Find him, no matter what the cost, I want to know where Michael Adams is!" Saying this, the man terminated the connection.

The man picked up a photo from the desk, a photo of Michael and looking at it, he said, "Where are you, Michael? We have some unfinished business."